Love ON THE *Slopes*

One Night to Forever, Book Four

MELISSA McCLONE

Cardinal Press, LLC
January 2019
ISBN-13: 9781944777241

Dedication

Thank you to Jack Strand and Kate Fraser
for giving me a peek into a ski racer's mind.

And a final thanks to my best friend, Debbie Bishko,
for putting up with my slow alpine skiing and not
laughing too hard when I tried cross-country skiing.

Prologue

Ryland "Ry" Guyer's head hurt. He squeezed his eyes tightly together, but that didn't stop him from feeling as if a figure skater were landing a triple axel on his skull, the blade slicing into his brain with talented precision.

How much had he drunk last night?

He rolled over in bed. *His* bed, he hoped.

Unsure of the time and where he was, Ry forced open his heavy eyelids. The light hurt, a hammer-slamming-against-his-forehead kind of pain, but the ceiling wasn't spinning. The walls didn't move, either.

Both were good signs. This wouldn't be a bad hangover.

He smiled. Didn't hurt. Another plus.

A white sheet covered him. No blankets, but he might have kicked them off. He didn't remember undressing or going to bed, but he often didn't after a night of partying.

Ry rose up on his elbows.

Sunlight streamed in through a crack in the curtains. He recognized the hotel room—his. A bag lay on the floor. His US Ski Team jacket hung on a chair.

Satisfaction filled him. He'd earned his place on the team. He was twenty-three with a silver and a bronze medal from the recent Winter Games in Sochi. His parents and their wealth hadn't made that happen. He had, with sweat, hard work, and a touch of luck. Nothing could take away his accomplishments.

Whoa. He did a double take.

Who was the cute girl asleep in the other chair?

She seemed familiar as did the clothes she wore. He squinted. The long-sleeved T-shirt and sweatpants belonged to him but looked better on her.

Hot.

Too bad he didn't remember her name or fooling around with her last night.

No problem. He would make up for the lost memories with a not-so-lazy morning in bed. After he brushed his teeth. His mouth tasted like he'd been sucking on a skater's sweaty foot.

He got out of bed and stretched.

"You're awake," a soft, feminine voice said.

Ry faced her. "So are you."

Her dark-blond hair fell past her shoulders. A charming pink colored her cheeks. Pretty brown eyes stared at him with adoration.

Ry's chest puffed with pride. He loved being someone's idol. Not wanting to disappoint her, he flashed a smile, his most charming one. "Good morning."

"Feel okay?" she asked, sounding concerned.

"Not too worse for the wear." He'd feel better once she was no longer wearing his clothes and in his bed. "Give me a minute. I'll be good to go again."

She stood. "Again?"

She might appear innocent, but she wouldn't be in his room the next morning if she didn't know how this worked. His clothes hung on her, but underneath had to be a tight body meant just for him. "You, me, between the sheets."

Her eyes widened. She took a deep breath, giving him a better view of her chest.

He might have been drunk, but he'd chosen wisely. He tried to remember her name. One popped into his tired brain. "Brittany from the C team, right?"

She shook her head. "Brynn. D team."

Cool. He'd scored a development babe who could

be a future alpine star.

"Sorry. A little hung over. I'm Ry. A team. But you probably know that." No worries about calling her Brittany. By the time sweet Brynn left his room, she would forget he hadn't known her name. "While I'm in the bathroom, get out of those clothes and into bed. We can get reacquainted."

Her mouth parted.

Nice lips. Kissable lips. Ones he wanted to taste and savor since he didn't remember their kisses from last night. "Be right back, Brynn."

See, he knew her name.

Damp clothes hung on the shower curtain rod. He and Brynn must have taken a walk or been rolling around in the snow. Not surprising. He breathed easier outside. Didn't matter if he was sober or drunk. Alone or with a beautiful woman.

On a mountain, Ry knew his purpose. No one was forcing him into a life he didn't want. He couldn't say that at his father's outdoor apparel company.

After Ry finished in the bathroom, he opened the door, eager to join Brynn in bed. "Ready?"

No answer.

"Don't be shy."

Silence.

"Brynn?"

He went around the corner. What the…?

The bed was empty. So was the chair.

And the room.

Weird. This wasn't normal. Usually, he had to kick out women. She must have gotten enough sex last night. Too bad he didn't remember because it was the quieter ones who always surprised him.

No big deal. Ry crawled into bed and pulled up the sheet. It was Brynn's loss for not wanting to go another round with him, but he hoped she returned his clothes and had taken nothing else from his room. He never wanted to find his stuff for sale on eBay again.

He'd learned the hard way that women weren't interested in love. They wanted a payout and would do anything to get one. Even if it meant lying and stealing and breaking hearts.

His heart.

Never again.

He took what women offered, never looking forward to the future or back into the past. Living in the present was the best way not to get hurt again.

Chapter One

Five years later

Pinks, oranges, and blues colored the early Monday morning sky over Sun Valley. Ry's boots sank into the snow. It was late March, and the Idaho weather was perfect. The cold air stung his lungs, a familiar feeling he relished. He'd been spending too much time in the gym and doing physical therapy. He belonged outside on a mountain, the place he called home.

"Going to be a bluebird day," he said to his friend

and US Ski Team member Chas Morris.

"Sunny skies. A dusting of powder. No lift lines." Smiling, Chas placed his skis on the snow. He was six foot two, an inch taller than Ry. "Nothing better."

Chas had won two gold medals at PyeongChang and was the top male alpine skier in the US. He'd flown in from Europe after the final World Cup race. He might be the definition of a champion, but he wouldn't be hauling in so many wins next season if Ry had his say. The two were friends and teammates, but also competitors. A good thing the podium was big enough for both of them.

A helmet covered Chas's reddish-brown hair. He stuck his poles under his arm. "Feel good to be here?"

"Yeah." The skis lying on the snow captured Ry's attention. The sense of longing, always present since his accident over two years ago, grew tenfold. "Just wish I could practice."

"You'll be tearing up the slopes soon enough."

This summer, according to his doctors. "I can't wait."

Since his ski crash during the downhill at St. Moritz, he'd faced numerous surgeries and rehab. His progress had been standing-still slow. He hadn't been able to compete at PyeongChang. Worse, he hadn't been able to do the one thing he loved more than anything—ski.

From the first time he'd strapped on skis at the age of four, skiing was all he'd wanted to do. All he'd done before destroying his right side.

"Until then, I'll cheer for you and the other old farts," he joked.

Chas made a face. "Some young ones want to chase us down to take their shot at making the national team, but I'm not ready for a walker yet."

"Just a ball and chain."

"You know it. Taylor is all mine."

"Keep rubbing it in."

"Sorry." Chas's smile spread to the edges of his helmet. "But she's…amazing."

The guy had it bad. Funny, given the number of women in and out of Chas's life over the years, but Ry was happy for his friend and for Taylor Bradshaw. The two world-class, gold- medal-winning skiers would make lightning-fast ski babies together.

"You're a lucky man," Ry said.

"Sure am." Chas kicked snow from his ski boots. "You're doing well for yourself. Heard you're dating another supermodel."

"Nah." Ry didn't want a girlfriend. Even a casual hookup would distract him from his recovery. No one knew he hadn't dated since his crash. Most assumed he was being discreet, not living like a monk, because of his reputation. He flexed his gloved fingers. "Strictly business."

"Come on. Every time I open a magazine, I see you with a living-my-best-life grin on your face and a beautiful woman hanging on your arm. You can't tell me nothing happens after the photographer leaves."

"I'm just earning my keep and helping out the team."

The US Ski Team was sponsored solely through donations—America's team in every sense of the word. Mugging for the camera allowed Ry to pay his own way while he healed. After his father offered to make a seven-figure donation to the team if Ry modeled, he'd become the face of Guyer Gear. Ry wanted to keep the family company separate from skiing, but the benefit to the team made it impossible for him to say no.

"Though I'll tell you"—he gave his friend a knowing look—"a photo shoot in a hot tub with a gorgeous model is hard work."

"Hardly working."

Ry rolled his eyes.

Chas laughed. "If there's no supermodel in your life, you'd better find yourself a snow bunny while you're here. The nights get chilly—"

"I'll be fine. Nothing like having a bed to yourself."

"Warm and not alone is better."

Ry was used to being alone these days. Some nights he didn't think about it much. Others, too much. But he'd made the right decision. The only choice. Reaching his goal was all that mattered. Coming back from injuries as serious as his wasn't easy, but he was driven. He might have a high-paying job waiting for him, but he wasn't ready to retire from competition yet. "I need to focus. Beijing is coming up."

"Not until 2022." Chas's brows drew together. "Three years is a long time."

"It's not that long."

One thought kept Ry going through the pain and the frustration of his injuries and recovery—the 2022 Winter Games in Beijing.

He'd been drinking the night before the race in St. Moritz. A stupid decision that could have killed him, all because he wanted to piss off his parents with his bad behavior—show his mom and dad they couldn't control every part of his life. But the only person Ry had hurt was himself.

Though the injuries from the crash had only been the first wake-up call. There'd been a second one months after that. It hadn't happened on skis but was way worse than his actual crash. One that had finally made him realize he was on the wrong path and put the partying lifestyle behind him. No alcohol or women. Some might call the lifestyle change rash, but he wouldn't argue with the results. He was in better shape today, injuries aside, than when he'd won two medals in Sochi. If he kept this up, he'd challenge Chas for the gold in 2022.

And win.

Resolve made Ry stand taller. "Three more years is nothing."

"When you decide you want more in your life…someone special—"

"I don't. Won't." *Can't.*

Winning a gold medal meant too much. Called for sacrifices. Ones he would gladly make before he took over the family company. That was his future. Guyer Gear. Until then, he wanted to make the most of the present.

With skiing, he could be himself, follow his passion and dreams. Here, he was Ry or Ry-Guy, not Ryland Guyer the Fourth, heir to Guyer Gear with the expectations of his entire family, generations living and dead, riding on his shoulders. The thought of being stuck behind a desk made him downright queasy, but he'd made a deal with his father and would do his part when the time came.

"Easy to say until you meet the right woman. Then, *bam.*" Chas secured his helmet strap. "She's all you can think about."

"Taylor."

Chas nodded once.

Not going to happen.

"I've never met a woman who made me feel that way." Ry had thought he'd found the one and bought her an engagement ring, but she'd been more interested in his family's money than in him. The devastating breakup and finding out she'd been stealing from him since the beginning of their relationship had led to his don't-care-party-hardy attitude at the age of twenty-one. He never wanted to put his happiness—and his heart—in someone else's hands. Best to focus on his goals. Next season would be his first on skis in over two years. He wanted to show the coaches he was serious about competing at an elite level again. Being cut from the team was not an option. Speaking of which… "You'd better get up top or Coach will chew you out."

Chas stepped on the skis. His boots clicked into the bindings.

The sound greeted Ry like a long-lost friend. He wanted to race again, feel the adrenaline pumping through his veins. Pushing himself to the edge to cut a hundredth of a second or tucking on a straightaway to go faster, finding the perfect line down the course and flying to the finish line.

Not being able to ski had left a huge gap in his life. He'd be happy to snowplow like a beginner down a green run serviced by a tow rope. Anything to feel the snow beneath his skis and the wind on his face.

"Yeah, Coach has been riled up." Chas lowered his goggles. "Don't need him on me more than he is."

"Tell the guys to kick your butt up there."

"As if they could."

"Just wait until *I'm* back."

Chas waved a pole. "Can't wait to beat you again."

"In your dreams." Ry headed toward the lodge, an inviting building constructed of logs and rock with paned glass windows. A large sun deck offered plenty of room for skiers to sit outside, but everyone was inside on this chilly morning.

Stragglers passed by on their way to the one lift operating for early practice runs.

"Guyer." Coach Mike Frederick's deep voice bellowed across the snow. Pushing sixty, the alpine men's head coach was solid and strong, a six-foot-tall wall of muscle. His steely-eyed gaze narrowed. "About time you showed up."

"The trainer had me in the pool first thing this morning and then sent me off to the gym to be tortured with a new killer workout."

"And?"

"I survived. Did better than expected." Ry pushed back his shoulders. "Should be ready for summer camp."

"Good. Chile and New Zealand haven't been the same without you."

During the summer and fall, the team trained in the southern hemisphere when snow was difficult to find closer to home. A feeling of pride flowed through Ry. "Looking forward to it."

"Excellent." Coach drove the team hard and demanded results, but he cared about each athlete. "I want you to work with a skier this week. Talented. Thought this would be a breakout season with her early World Cup results, but she lost focus. Talk to her. See if you can help her get back on track."

No wonder the coaches had asked him to come to Sun Valley for the final event of the season. To be honest, the call had surprised Ry. He'd been settling back into his rehab and training schedule following a photo shoot in LA and an impromptu stop in San Francisco to help out a friend of a friend. "Who is it?"

"Brynn Windham."

The name brought a rush of memories. Waking up with her in his hotel room, finding his sweatpants and shirt she'd been wearing, washed and folded, in a bag on his doorknob later that day, but the rest of their time together had been sucked into a black hole. He'd assumed what happened that night even if he hadn't remembered. Brynn, still on the team, had avoided him ever since as if he were radioactive.

"I'm not the right person for this." At team functions, she acknowledged his presence with a hard glare or the evil-eye, so he kept his distance. She'd done the same with him. "Taylor had trouble focusing last season before her knee injury. She'd be a better choice."

"Coach Tolliver agrees you're the one." Kate Tolliver was the women's head coach.

"But—"

"Wes thinks so, too." Assistant Coach Wes Smith's friendly teddy bear personality was the opposite of the men's head coach's grizzly demeanor. "What you've been through since St. Moritz makes you the perfect one to help Brynn."

"When was she injured?"

"Her issues aren't physical, but they've been as debilitating to her success. Brynn has the speed, but since December, she's dropped from the top of the standings to the bottom. She needs to pull herself together. We downsized the team last year. There may be more cuts."

Next season's preliminary team nominations would be announced in May. To be nominated, skiers had to meet the set criteria for their team level—A, B, C, and Development. Brynn's spot must be in jeopardy because she didn't meet the requirements, or the coaches were unsure about granting a discretionary selection to keep her on the team.

A shiver shot down Ry's spine. An injury discretion would put him on the team for the upcoming season. But if he didn't rank high enough this time next year, he would find himself in a similar place as Brynn.

Still, he hesitated. "She may not want my help."

"You two have a history?"

Crack. The sharp sound filled the air. An icicle dropped from an eave. "More like a mistake. We put it behind us."

At least Ry had. He'd never spoken to Brynn again, so he didn't know how she felt.

"No problem then," Coach said in a matter-of-fact tone.

His voice might as well be a judge's gavel

signaling a verdict. No appeal. Sentence nonnegotiable. Ry swallowed. "Guess we'll find out."

Coach handed him a US Ski Team lanyard. "This will give you access to places Brynn might want to go."

Ry studied the *team assistant* badge. An odd taste, like he'd chewed moldy bread, coated his mouth. He preferred wearing an athlete's lanyard.

"I'll send Brynn into the cafeteria after practice," Coach said. "Wait for her there."

Ry's throat clogged. The team had stood by him. The least he could do was talk to Brynn. He placed the lanyard into his jacket pocket. "Okay."

"Thanks."

He hadn't expected gratitude from the in-your-face coach who had developed him into a champion and been at his bedside when Ry had woken up from his first surgery. "Wait until you see what happens before you thank me."

He might crash and burn worse with Brynn Windham than he had at St. Moritz.

Chapter Two

Brynn's snow boots clomped against the day lodge floor like cement blocks. She'd changed out of her practice gear but moved slow, trying not to limp. Her hip ached. She'd caught an edge, and the fresh snow couldn't cushion the hard fall. Her bruise, however, hadn't hurt as much as Coach Frederick yelling at her and then telling her to talk to Ryland Guyer. She'd skied straight to Coach Tolliver and asked if she had to speak with him. Tolliver had said *do it*.

An elephant pressed on Brynn's chest. Anxiety

spiraled.

Not what she needed before a make-or-break competition.

Don't panic.

A few minutes spent with the last person she wanted to talk to again wouldn't matter. She needed to grab a coffee first. The heat would warm her. The caffeine would clear her head.

She needed a podium finish in the super combined. No, a win.

W-I-N.

In both the downhill and slalom portions to prove she should stay on the team.

So what if she'd had the worst season ever? Finishing a race had become a reason to celebrate, no matter what place she ended up in the standings. People whispered her career was over. Washed up at twenty-four. She hadn't met the team criteria though she'd been close. Many assumed her name would be left off the upcoming season's nomination list.

No giving up.

Skiing was her life, and the US Ski Team was her family. The only one she had left besides two of her siblings. Forget the place she used to call home with her mom, dad, and five older brothers. That no longer existed, never had really. She couldn't lose her spot on the team.

Wouldn't.

A solid showing might earn her a coach's

discretion and keep her on the team. That meant racing her best this week. She didn't need help from Guyer. She pulled off her gloves and shoved them into her parka's pockets.

Her cell phone buzzed. She read the text.

Jax: *How did practice go?*

Of course her brother would be checking up on her. Better answer or he would call. She typed a reply.

Brynn: *Cold, but good.*
Jax: *Everything else okay?*

Her heart squeezed. No, but she couldn't tell him the truth. She hated keeping secrets from her brothers, Jax and Ace. She'd always been closest to them, the two youngest of the five boys. Both played professional hockey, Jax for the NHL and Ace for the AHL. They had no trouble dragging problems out of her, even long distance, but this time, Brynn had to manage without their advice. She typed.

Brynn: *All is well. Ready to race.*
Jax: *Great. Time to hit the ice.*

Her brother must have practice. She tucked the phone into her pocket.

"Brynn."

Chills shot down her arms. Guyer.

Ryland Guyer had broken her heart when she was nineteen, crumbling the pedestal she'd put him on and turning her crush on him to dust. He'd been twenty-three, fresh from medaling at the Games in Sochi and hot, oh-so-hot. He'd seemed perfect. A Prince Charming, who slayed black diamond slopes.

Only he wasn't.

She'd been naïve, taking him to his room when she'd found him outside in the falling snow, but he'd been so drunk she'd worried about leaving him alone. She'd been young and stupid then. Way too starstruck and trusting. Lesson learned. One she'd shared with female teammates. A few others had a drunk Ry-Guy story. Only none of them had had their reputation ruined by his lies about what had happened in the hotel room that night.

Such a jerk.

"Brynn," he repeated.

Pressing her lips together, she squared her shoulders and turned toward his voice. Her gaze collided with blue eyes, beautiful ones surrounded by thick lashes. His all-American good looks, the kind found on movie screens and glossy magazine covers, were more appealing than ever. No man had a right to be so attractive. A scruff of whiskers gave his handsome face a rugged edge.

Sexy.

Her pulse kicked up, racing as if she were

speeding down the mountain, not standing inside a warm lodge with the aroma of coffee lingering in the air.

Stop.

No reason to overreact. He hadn't changed. Pretty packaging, yes, but remove the wrapping and nothing was underneath but a rock-hard body. He was a player. Zero heart and compassion. A guy who thought she'd had sex with him once and would again when he hadn't even remembered her name.

Loser.

And a liar.

Waiting, he stared at her.

Oh, yeah. Her turn to speak.

Brynn cleared her thick throat. "Hey."

Guyer sat at a table by himself. His brown hair was longer than the short style he usually wore. His sweater showed off wide shoulders. Maybe the navy color was why his eyes appeared bluer. The lines around the corners of his eyes were more visible. Hard living did that to a person. Not that she cared what he did to himself unless his actions affected the team.

"Did Coach Frederick talk to you?" Guyer asked.

"Yes, but—"

He laughed.

The wicked sound curled her toes, annoying her more. She shouldn't be reacting to him.

"I knew there would be a *but*," he said.

Her hands balled. "Still full of yourself."

"Better than being empty." He motioned to the spot across the table from him. "Have a seat."

"I prefer to stand."

"The coaches are here."

Tolliver could be hard-nosed, but the coach knew when to push and when to let up. Frederick seemed to search for a reason to get on skiers, but he wouldn't find one now. Brynn sat. "I didn't think they'd check to see if I showed up."

"Frederick wants us to talk."

Why? Guyer might be an expert in picking up women, hiding hangovers from the coaches, and lying to impress others, but Brynn wasn't interested in learning those tricks. "You haven't competed in over two years, so I'm not sure how you can help me."

"I competed nonstop before my injury." His voice took on a defensive tone. "The coaches haven't competed in years, but they know what they're talking about."

"You're moving into coaching?"

"No." The one word spoke volumes. "Coach asked me, so here I am."

The coaches wanted this, so Brynn would play along though she didn't know why she tried so hard with Frederick. He was distant and unemotional, never pleased with what she and her teammates accomplished. In some ways, he reminded her of her father, Sully, who coached minor league hockey in the

American Hockey League.

Every muscle tensed.

He had never forgiven her for being a girl. She'd screwed his chance to field a hockey team of sons. The first of many failures he had never let her forget. When he traveled on long road trips when she was a kid, her brothers missed him so much. Not Brynn. That was the only time she could relax and not be compared to her five older brothers.

He'd seemed clueless on how to bond with a daughter. Whenever her school had a father-daughter dance, he would be too busy to attend. No matter what she did—no matter how many Father's Day, birthday, and good luck cards she made him—he remained detached. As she'd found out in December, her being a girl wasn't the only barrier to their relationship.

Yeah, he and Coach Frederick had a lot in common, including Brynn's mom.

She blew out a puff of air. "Let's get this over with."

Silence.

Brynn shouldn't have expected anything else from Guyer. She fought the urge to bolt, but knowing the coaches were nearby kept her seated in the chair. "So…"

Guyer pushed one of the two coffee cups on the table toward her. "For you. Two sugars and a dash of cream."

That was how she drank hers. Her mouth watered, but she squinted. "Never saw you as the stalker type."

"I'm usually being stalked," he admitted. "But you can learn almost anything in less than five minutes on the internet. Your favorite color is orange?"

"Yes, the brighter the better." Brynn sipped her coffee. The liquid was hot and sweet, the way she liked it. "Why did you go to the trouble to do a search on me?"

"If we're going to work together—"

"Stop." She raised her left hand, palm facing him. "Neither of us wants to work together, so let's not pretend otherwise."

He didn't contradict her. Brynn wasn't surprised, but she didn't appreciate the sting of disappointment that came out of the blue. "Give me some advice now, and we'll call it good."

"That's not what Coach has in mind."

"He'll never know."

"Yes, he will."

Guyer tapped his fingers on the table. His nails were clean and in better shape than hers. Then again, he'd been modeling, according to her roommate, Lila Raines, so maybe manicures were part of his photo shoot prep.

"Coach knows everything," Guyer added.

Far from it. Frederick might know skiing, but he was clueless about other stuff. But no one else knew that except Brynn.

She wrapped her hand around the coffee cup. The warmth didn't take away the chill. "The coaches want to say they did everything they could before I'm cut from the team. Everyone knows I don't meet the selection criteria for a nomination. My only hope is a coach's discretion spot."

She expected Guyer to show a sign of relief—he'd avoided her over the years the way she had him—but his expression didn't change.

He picked up his coffee. "I didn't know until this morning."

"You haven't been around."

"I'm here now." He raised his coffee. "Don't make this a wasted trip for me. My dad let me take the company jet so I could fly direct and bypass the drive from Boise."

"Rough life."

"Doesn't suck." Ry took a sip. "So Coach said you're not injured. That means something's going on in your head. Have any idea what?"

"Everyone who's tried to help me has come up empty." Of course, she hadn't told them the reason she'd lost her focus. She'd promised her mother not to tell anyone and hadn't. Couldn't. "We're talking sports psychologists, counselors, coaches. The best around."

A part of Brynn wished someone could help her, but telling the truth might get her kicked off the team faster than having poor race results. She didn't dare.

"Why do you think you can do better?" she asked.

"Don't know if I can, but Coach wants me to try. If you're not interested, that's fine, but I won't lie to him about what we're doing."

"Why not? You used to lie all the time." His lies had been infamous and used in a drinking game. Something to joke and laugh about until he'd spread lies about the two of them having sex. Suddenly, people viewed her differently. And not in a good way.

Denying the rumors had made her appear guilty and heartbroken over Ry-Guy. Granted, only the younger guys had expected her to put out, but she hadn't appreciated the curious looks she'd received from others, including the team staff.

Guyer's mouth tightened. "I don't do a lot of things I used to do."

Her curiosity piqued, she drank more coffee to keep from asking him questions.

"What happened in Åre?" he asked.

His question about the race in Sweden was unexpected. Unwelcome, too.

Memories careened through her head like a possessed jackhammer, the noise more deafening than the cheering crowds at the finish line. "I had a bad run."

"More than one. You were DQ'd in multiple events."

She stared into her cup. "Everyone has a bad

competition."

"You've had an off season."

Her muscles tensed, knotting themselves like the tangled fringe on her old scarf. She'd had a chance to finish on the podium at Lake Louise the week before Are but hadn't. Her loss caused "Dad" to go off on her. She'd tried her entire life to prove herself to Sully, to earn his love, to make him as proud of her as he was of her hockey-playing brothers. At least she'd discovered why pleasing him had been an impossible task. Sully wasn't her biological father.

"I'm doing the best I can," she said finally.

"You believe that?"

"No." She might be withholding the truth, but she wasn't a liar. "Or I wouldn't be here with you."

A smile spread across Guyer's face. "A sense of humor is good, but so is being focused. I watched a few clips of your recent races. You've lost your focus."

"Yes." But she couldn't say why. Brynn gnawed on her lower lip.

"Do you want to stay on the team?" he asked.

"Yes." The word catapulted from her mouth. "More than anything."

Doubt filled his gaze.

"It's true." She sounded defensive and on guard, exactly how she felt. "I'll do whatever it takes."

"Does that include working with me?"

Brynn didn't reply. Instead, she sipped her coffee.

"You were skiing great until the middle of December," he added. "Something changed."

Finding out about her mother's past affair with Coach Mike Frederick was the *something*. Brynn's world had collapsed and poor skiing had been the result.

Not that she blamed anyone. How could she?

Her mom was a quiet woman, attractive but browbeaten in a family of athletic, active boys, with a distant husband who lived and breathed hockey. She'd put aside her ski racing dreams and never mentioned the sport until enrolling Brynn in ski lessons. Turned out her mom had dated Coach when they were younger. They'd reconnected twenty-five years ago at a wedding for a mutual skier friend and slept together after the reception. Brynn had been the result.

Bet Grandma had no idea what happened that weekend she watched the five boys.

Sully didn't know who Brynn's birth father was, but he put his name on her birth certificate. Part of his and her mother's deal when they agreed to stay together after both had cheated—Sully during multiple road trips and her mother at the wedding.

No one was supposed to know Brynn was the result of her mother's affair.

When Brynn had discovered the truth due to a slip of the tongue, she'd begged her mom to tell her more, and her mother had, not in detail, but enough so Brynn knew the circumstances of her conception.

Only two people knew the identity of Brynn's father—she and her mother. Coach Frederick had no idea her mom had gotten pregnant. She'd asked him never to contact her because she wanted to make her marriage work for her children's sake.

"At Åre, you didn't lose your focus, you fell apart," Guyer continued. "Imploded like a snowball against a brick wall."

She peered over the lip of her cup. "Gee, thanks."

"Am I wrong?"

Brynn hesitated. "No."

"Did some guy break your heart? Dwyer?"

"Puh-leeze." Jon Dwyer was a teammate and Guyer clone who treated women as sexual objects, was a player extraordinaire, and should be avoided at all costs. She lowered her cup. "Give me some credit."

"Tell me what's going on so I can help."

Brynn couldn't tell him. Her five older brothers had no idea she was their half sister. Her mom had admitted being worried about the fallout if the truth came out. The family would be split down the middle.

Her mother had promised Sully to never see Brynn's father again and hadn't. She'd also promised that Brynn would have no contact with her birth father though that had been out of her mother's control once Brynn moved up on the national team. If Sully found out Coach Frederick was her father and had become a regular part of Brynn's life, who knew what he'd do? As for her brothers...

Ace and Jax would take their mom's side—and Brynn's. The two had a complicated relationship with Sully. Her brothers' teams weren't in the same franchise or in Jax's case league as Sully's, but their father was competitive about everything. The oldest three, who were entrenched in their careers and families and especially close to their father, would take their dad's. Eli worked for Sully. He would do whatever his dad asked, including keeping his kids away from their grandmother. Grandchildren were her mom's pride and joy. Her mom didn't want to risk family turmoil and not being able to see them.

"No worries." Brynn's insides shook, but she feigned confidence. Something she'd been doing since December. A lot longer if she thought about her childhood. "I've got this."

"And if you don't?"

Being on this team meant everything to Brynn. After feeling ignored and thinking something was wrong with her, she'd found herself on the slopes, a drive to make something of herself, a confidence to go fast and never back down. She didn't know who she was outside of skiing. Even though the last thing she felt was indifferent, she shrugged. "I'll be fine."

At least I hope so.

"Brynn..."

The urgency in his voice prickled her skin. She didn't need pity. Not from him.

Go. Now.

Her instincts had never failed her. They wouldn't this time. She pushed away from the table and stood.

Ouch. Standing made her hip throb. Another reason to leave. She needed to ice the bruise from her fall this morning.

Brynn didn't glance at Guyer. "I've got to go."

Chapter Three

This was worse than Ry imagined. Breakfast and another coffee sounded good, but he needed to go after Brynn. Eager to find her, he strode out of the day lodge. He wouldn't call her a hot mess, but she was heading in that direction. She was also in full denial as he'd been.

The sun shone bright in the blue sky, but the wind had picked up. He zipped his jacket, put on a beanie, and shoved his hands into gloves.

Skiers passed him, loaded down with skis, boots, and bags. A man carried three pairs of skis while two smiling kids shuffled beside him. One boy, around four, wore a blue parka with golden flames on the sleeves. Guyer Gear's double G emblem was on the coat and coordinating ski pants. The kid kept pointing every which way, overflowing with excitement.

As Ry watched the trio pass, he remembered the ski trips when he'd been a little kid and how his dad had shared his love of the sport. He'd do the same when he had children. Not that he wanted a family anytime soon, but someday.

Being on the mountain with his dad had been the best time. Much better than when Ry was older and the only thing his dad wanted to share with him was work.

As Brynn walked twenty feet ahead, her ponytail bounced.

He quickened his pace to catch up, mindful of each step with his right foot. Habit, one he hoped to put behind him when his leg completely healed.

She'd put on a good act in the lodge, but he saw through the "I've got this" bravado. The slight quiver of her bottom lip, the tightness around her mouth, and the worry in her eyes gave her away. Brynn believed she could tackle this on her own, but she couldn't.

She picked up a pink glove that a little girl had dropped. The child's mother thanked her, and Brynn was off again.

Seeing her was like staring at his reflection after

being injured. For the first six months of his recovery, he'd acted the same. Same denial. Same mask of confidence when he'd never been so frightened in his life.

Then he'd hit rock bottom.

That collapse had jolted him worse than crashing out during the race in St. Moritz. But he was lucky. Friends had rallied around him, ignoring his demands for them to go away. They hadn't listened.

Neither would he.

Brynn was stuck with him whether or not she had her own support network. He might not solve her problems, but she couldn't race much worse this week than she'd been doing.

Ry cut the distance between them. Brynn's pace was off, her gait stiff. No limp, but she favored her left side.

"Brynn," he called out. "Wait up."

Peering over her shoulder, she blew out a long breath that floated on the cold air. "Seriously?"

"Can't get rid of me that easily."

Her lips pressed together, the corners curved downward. The wind toyed with the stray tendrils of hair, whipping a few across her face. She was attractive, maybe more so than she'd been at nineteen. Same brown eyes, tan skin, and lips made for long, slow kisses.

Something was different, though.

She may have avoided him, but even from a

distance, her eagerness and excitement about skiing had been contagious during team meetings. He'd appreciated that about her even if she hadn't liked him. Now, she appeared weary and defeated.

Something had happened. Something not good.

After his injury, he'd realized how little he controlled in his life. That had been a rude and disturbing awakening. Maybe she'd come to the same understanding.

He stood next to her.

"What?" Brynn sounded annoyed.

"You don't want my help."

"Give the man a gold star. Or would that be a gold medal?"

Her words stung. The elusive gold was the carrot driving him, but he wouldn't react and give her what she wanted. Instead, he took a calming breath. "If I apologize…?"

"A little late, don't you think?"

She had a point, but he needed to say something. "You were young, new to the team. Having a one-night stand was a mistake."

She stared at him as if he'd morphed into a green alien with one eye and a dozen antennae sticking out of his head. "Nothing you say should surprise me, but this does."

She sounded disgusted, not annoyed, but he didn't understand why. "What did I say?"

"We didn't"—her voice was low as if telling a

secret—"*have* a one-night stand."

"Yes, we did."

"No, we did not even though you told everyone we had." She pinned him with a hard-as-steel gaze. If looks could kill, he'd be six feet under. "Do you remember *anything* about that night?"

"I woke up in bed." He kept his voice quiet so as not to draw attention, but the people around them seemed more interested in getting to the slopes. "You were in my room, wearing my clothes."

"But that doesn't mean we had…sex." She whispered the last word.

"Then why was I naked?"

She wet her lips. "Because I had to undress you after you threw up on both of us."

The night remained a blank.

"I changed into clothes I found in your bag and then washed the dirty stuff in the tub," she continued. "I left yours to dry in the bathroom. Mine were hanging in the closet so I wouldn't forget them."

"I don't remember."

"A memory lapse didn't stop you from talking about me to the others, telling them how good I was in bed. That I did whatever you asked me to do."

Ry swore. He'd been young and stupid—a selfish jerk. He could imagine himself doing that. Sad but true. "I wouldn't have lied."

She raised a brow, giving him a dubious look.

"I might have filled in the gaps," he added.

"You blacked out. The entire night was a gap."

He'd treated her badly, and she was responding. He deserved her harsh tone. "Yes, but everyone thought... I assumed—"

"Bad assumption. And I paid the price. Well, my reputation did, and what the guys my age expected if we went out. Needless to say, not dating was easier." Holding her chin high, Brynn crossed her arms in front of her chest. "For the record, you kissed me once. Then you got sick. I cleaned you up. You passed out. End of the story until you woke up the next morning."

What she said replayed through his mind. Worse, he could imagine that happening. He'd never been good at drinking in moderation. This also explained her reaction to him all these years.

He wasn't proud of how he'd acted. He'd ended up with a hangover, a small price to pay, compared to her having to deal with what he'd told others. Not that he remembered doing that, either.

Nothing he did or said would make this right, but he had to try.

"Too late, I realize, but I'm sorry." Ry hoped he sounded sincere because he *was* sorry. "I made assumptions about us. You. It's not an excuse, but I partied too much. Took advantage of women. Spouted off my big mouth. I was a complete jerk. But I'm not that same guy."

"Sure, you're not." Her disbelief cut like a newly

sharpened ski edge.

"It's true." And Ry knew what to do. He would make amends for his past actions by helping Brynn beat whatever was messing with her head. "I can't change what happened, but I'm here now. Let me help you get through this competition."

She rolled her eyes, but she didn't take off. "That's guilt talking."

"I won't deny that. I'm probably the last person you'd want help from."

"Not 'probably.' You *are*."

Hearing that poked at him like the tip of a ski pole being pressed against his chest, but he wouldn't be deterred. "The coaches think I'm the right person to work with you for a reason."

"Yeah, so you can lead me down the dark path, so I screw up more and get kicked off the team."

"No freakin' way." Anger burned in his gut. His hands balled. "Not being able to do what you love sucks. I'm there now. I'd never take someone away from her passion. Especially skiing. Never."

The doubt remained on her face.

His fault.

Which meant he had to make things right between them.

A bus parked at the curb, and people streamed out, talking and laughing while they waited for their skis and boots to be unloaded. He needed to convince Brynn to let him help her. Telling her what he'd gone through would do it, but this wasn't the place to talk with so many around.

"Let's head over to where I'm staying," Ry suggested. "We can talk while you ice your hip. Did you catch an edge?"

"How did you know?"

"Been there, done that more times than I want to count." He motioned for her to follow. "Come on. I've got everything you need to make you feel better."

She raised her chin. "Is that one of your pickup lines?"

"It was once, but not now. This is a legit offer."

She stared down her nose. "I don't believe you."

Man, she had the haughty expression down. Not that he blamed her. "If you'd rather talk to the team doc—"

"No." The word flew from her mouth faster than a racer out of the starting gate. "Where's your place?"

Smiling would only upset her more so he didn't. "Not far."

She'd have plenty of time to throw more verbal jabs his way, and he deserved every single one. He wanted her to get them out, to speak her mind and call him names. Maybe then she'd listen to him, because she needed to hear what he had to say, or she might as well forget skiing and go home.

"The condo is less than a block away." Ry pointed to the complex up ahead. Brynn was trying to ignore her bruise, but he could tell from the way her hand hovered above her hip, it hurt. "My friends, Brett and Laurel Matthews, own it. He manages my investment portfolio."

Brynn shot him sideways glances. None were dagger-filled, so that was an improvement over previous encounters, though he doubted any of her thoughts about him were good. But he'd earned her dislike. That was on him.

Inside the unit, she glanced around. "Nice place."

"It's close to the slopes and comfortable." The one-story, two-bedroom condo was small and cozy. He'd expected Brett to own something fancier given the guy's business and net worth, but then Ry realized Brett and Laurel probably wanted a more homey vacation property now that they had little Noelle. They didn't need another showplace like their estate in Portland to impress people and clients.

Not that this unit was anywhere close to slumming. Laurel, an interior designer, had overseen the remodel and decorating. A granite breakfast bar with three stools separated the kitchen from the living room. A rock fireplace was along the left wall, and a dining area sat on the far side of the condo. The open floor plan and overstuffed furniture were perfect for relaxing.

Brynn sat on the couch and took off her snow boots, but she kept on her jacket, as if wanting to be ready to make a quick exit.

He hung his coat on the barstool and turned on

the gas fireplace. That would make her sorry she hadn't removed her coat. A childish move, maybe, but the way she looked down at him bugged Ry. Yes, he hadn't treated her well, but he wasn't the same person he'd been five years ago. If she wanted to sweat, that was her choice. Taking off her jacket wasn't a sign of surrender.

"I've got ice or frozen peas," he said from the adjoining kitchen.

"Peas, please." She rested her sock-covered foot on the coffee table.

He wrapped a bag in a dishtowel. "Hurting?"

"Not bad."

"Bet you've got a big bruise." He went into the living room. "Let me see."

Brynn stiffened. "Only if you want a knee in your groin."

Ry could do without her attitude. "Here are your peas."

She placed the pack against her hip. "Got ibuprofen?"

"Of course." He poured her a glass of water, grabbed the bottle from the bathroom, and handed them to her. "Want anything else?"

"Nope." She downed the pills. "The cold feels good."

"Did the doc or trainer examine you?"

She nodded once. "I'll be rechecked when I do dryland training."

A bruise wouldn't stop a skier from working out in the gym, but Ry hoped she was telling the truth about seeking medical attention. Though at this point in the season, joints and muscles might hurt with or without a fall.

He sat next to her but kept space between them. He didn't want her to think he was making a move. He wouldn't. Not even if he wanted a date, which he didn't. Brynn Windham was as prickly as a porcupine. She was acting this way because of him, but still…

"If you're hungry, I can order food," he offered.

"I'm not. What did you want to talk about?"

She wasn't wasting time. Then again, the super combined was in two days, followed by the super G, slalom, parallel slalom, and giant slalom.

"Me," he said.

She sighed.

"And you," he added. "I want you to know why I can help."

She adjusted a throw pillow behind her. "This should be good."

Not good, but necessary. He didn't share this side of his injury. Only those closest to him and his medical team had witnessed his meltdown and his struggles. But he had to tell Brynn so she would understand.

Ry took a breath and exhaled slowly. People saw him as happy-go-lucky, born with a silver spoon, out for a good time. He'd been that way before.

Now…not so much. "The coaches asked me to help you because I've been where you are. After my injury, I went through a…rough time."

"You were hurt. Unable to compete in PyeongChang."

Her voice sounded concerned, almost compassionate. Two emotions Ry hadn't expected from her. Nor did he deserve them.

"Most people would be upset," she added.

"Yes, but I lost it. Emotionally. The mental stuff piled on top of the physical." He cringed at the bad memories. "It was a mess."

She leaned toward him. "What happened?"

"I closed up and shut down. Before my crash, I might have been careless, sometimes thoughtless, even reckless, but never mean. I was then. I tried to drive away friends, make them hate me so they'd leave me alone in my misery. At my lowest point, I made my mother cry and cursed at my father. I'll never forget when my dad asked me what I'd done to their son Ryland. And that was before we'd resolved our differences."

"You had problems with your parents?"

"Big ones." He imagined his dad now with a smile on his face. Much better than the frowns Ry used to get. "My dad introduced me to skiing when I was four, but he didn't support my competing because he wanted me to work for him. He saw the Sochi Winter Games as my last hurrah, but I saw it as the beginning of something bigger for my skiing. I wanted another chance at a gold medal."

"That had to be tough."

Ry nodded. "The arguments started when I was eighteen. I felt I was being forced into a life I didn't want and rebelled. Drinking and partying helped me escape the future my father wanted for me. I rationalized my behavior by thinking if my reputation were bad enough he wouldn't want me to take over the company."

She didn't say anything, but her brows knotted as if she were considering what he'd said. "And now?"

"Crashing out made us see we were both wrong. My dad realized he shouldn't replace my dream with his. We came to an understanding. He would support my skiing one hundred percent, and I'd work full-time for the company after I retire from competition. Until then, I'll learn about the business and do what I can."

"And be the face of Guyer Gear?"

Ry nodded. Admitting this to a woman who hated him wasn't easy, but he felt compelled to continue. He owed Brynn for treating her so badly. She needed to understand that she wasn't the only skier who had issues. "My parents were only one part of this. I couldn't see what I was doing to them, my friends, and myself. I knew something wasn't right, but I didn't know how to fix it."

Brynn inhaled, and then she rubbed her lips together.

"Sound a little familiar?" he asked.

"Maybe."

Ry would take that as a yes.

"My right side was shattered. So was my spirit." He hated remembering the chaotic mix of emotions and the downward spiral, but he forced himself to continue for Brynn's sake. "I'd realized how little control I had over what happened. Nothing I did made a difference. I struggled to get through each day and night, overwhelmed with negative thoughts and nightmares. The voices in my head wouldn't shut up. I felt like the sun had vanished, swallowed up by this dark cloud that was never going away."

"Thunder, lightning, and a downpour of biblical proportions."

"Exactly." He leaned against the couch. "I was drenched. Weighted down to the point I wanted to give up."

Her gaze locked on his.

Something passed between them. Something strong. Something full of energy.

Understanding, perhaps? Yes, that had to be it.

"But you didn't," she said finally.

"People wouldn't let me, but if I'd tried to handle this on my own, I don't know where I'd be today." He took a breath. And another. "The drinking got worse. I was on pain meds, too. If I wasn't drunk, I was high. Sometimes both, and that led to an accidental overdose. I nearly died, but my friend

Henry, who I thought I'd pushed away for good, found me. Called for help."

"Ry…"

"I don't want your pity." The words rushed out. He couldn't help it. "Hitting rock bottom was the best thing that ever happened to me. It was the wake-up call I needed. Otherwise, I'd probably be dead."

He had to keep talking before he lost his nerve.

"It hasn't been easy. I'm not on skis yet. But I'm stronger than I was before my crash, both physically and mentally." He'd said the same thing to friends, family, and doctors, proven himself during workouts with physical therapists and top athletic trainers, but he wouldn't know if that was true until he was skiing again. Brynn, however, didn't need to know that. "If I can do this, so can you."

She flinched. Her lips parted. "Our situations are different. You were trying to live up to your dad's expectations and then you were critically injured. It's no wonder you needed to numb yourself with drugs and alcohol. My situation is…personal."

That was more info than Ry knew when they'd started but still not enough. He didn't know her, but he wished he did. He touched her shoulder. A show of support, yes, but also a way to feel connected. He needed that. Maybe she did, too.

"I have no idea what's going on in your life, or what's messing with your head, but whatever it is, you're not alone. People care about you. The coaches wouldn't have asked me to come to Sun Valley if they didn't want you to succeed."

Her eyes gleamed. "You think?"

Ry swore silently. He hadn't wanted to make her cry. He squeezed her shoulder. Well, her puffy jacket. "I know."

She blinked. "To be honest, I don't think anyone can help me, but I wouldn't want either of us to be in trouble with the coaches."

Not the resounding *yes* Ry wanted to hear, but that beat a *get lost*.

A smile tugged on the corners of his mouth. "Good, because I've been on Coach's naughty list for too long."

Her mouth slanted into a slight frown. "You might have a reserved spot. Old habits are difficult to break."

That was the truth. "I'm working on it."

"Try harder."

A coldness settled in his core. Ry got she didn't like him—Brynn had made that clear—but she didn't need to be rude about it. He was here to help. Or at the minimum, try. Not an easy task when she wouldn't tell him what was wrong. "I am."

Her gaze sharpened before lowering to her shoulder. "You're still touching me."

Ry jerked his arm away as if burned by fire. "Sorry."

And he was. He hadn't realized his hand was still

on her.

Weird. He'd been careful around women since his accident, not wanting them to think he was hitting on them. It had also been a way of keeping himself safe. So far his resolve to limit distractions had been working. He wanted that to continue, especially with her.

She studied him. "You're not how I remember."

"Neither are you."

"You don't remember anything about me."

"I remember you asleep in a chair and you leaving without saying goodbye." He also recalled her hero worship expression and being attracted to her. "That hurt."

"You called me Brittany and thought I'd still want to have sex with you." She leaned away from him. "How do you think *I* felt?"

Good point. He needed to consider what happened from her point of view. "I may have been a little arrogant."

"Little isn't the adjective I'd use." She didn't sound amused. "Then or now."

Brynn wasn't out to impress him. If anything, she would prefer if he left her alone. Ry appreciated knowing where he stood with her. "One of these days, you'll say something nice about me."

"Don't count on that being soon."

"It'll happen." Ry stretched out his legs. "I told you my story. Tell me yours."

"Not now." She placed the peas on the table and put on her boots. "Icing helped, but I need to check in with the trainer. Do a short workout."

He wasn't about to let her run away again. "I'll go with you."

"Nice of you to offer, but even though you know everyone, without a badge—"

"We're in luck." Ry stood, went over to his jacket, and pulled the lanyard from the pocket. "I'm a team assistant this week."

Her face pinched, full of tension and frustration, as if she'd been expecting to eat an orange but bit into a lemon.

Ry had surprised her. Good, because she kept shocking him. But he would be polite. "Something wrong?"

Her lower lip stuck out in an adorable almost-pout. "No."

"Then let's go."

Chapter Four

After a brief workout, Brynn iced her hip. She never thought she'd have anything in common with Ryland Guyer. She wanted to hate him, but his telling her what he'd been through tugged at her heart. A part of her wanted to help him, make sure he was okay, not headed in the wrong direction to the dark place he'd once been. Over the past three months, her emotions could swing from good to bad in an instant. At times, something inconsequential to most people would make her want to curl up in the fetal position and cry. Maybe Ry was beyond that back-and-forth when breathing took effort. She hoped so for his sake.

An unexpected reaction given their past, but his openness had surprised her. So had his experience because he seemed indestructible—or had until his crash. Hearing his story made her feel not so alone, but their situations were nothing alike. He wouldn't be able to help her. No one could.

Which didn't bode well for her upcoming races.

Think positively.

That was all she could do. Unfortunately.

After working on Brynn's hip, Amelia, one of the team's trainers, rubbed her shoulder.

Ry chatted with skiers, spotting for a couple of them lifting weights. He knew everyone. Not surprising since he'd been on the team for over a decade.

Amelia's fingers pressed and kneaded Brynn's muscles. The trainer was a favorite among the female teammates. No one got rid of cramps, including menstrual ones, as well as Amelia. "Better?"

"Yes."

Ry spoke to Sam Crawford, one of the A team skiers. Lila had a big crush on the guy. Which meant her roommate extolled Sam's virtues and race results day and night. A good thing he was a nice guy even if he treated Lila more like a kid sister than a potential love interest.

"Your muscles are so tight." Amelia massaged

Brynn's biceps. "Did you land on your entire side?"

"Just my hip."

Ry's laughter carried across the room, above the music, conversations, and exercise machines. She didn't know why she recognized the sound or liked it.

"Relax," Amelia said.

"I'm trying." Tough to do when Ryland Guyer was on Brynn's mind.

I don't do a lot of things I used to do.

Was that true?

She hadn't seen him around, other than at team meetings and events, because she'd done her best to avoid him, afraid she might cause a scene and resurrect the lies about them and that night. But she couldn't deny he was acting differently. The Ryland she remembered was charming and full of himself, God's gift to skiing and women. Being sober or getting older might account for the changes.

Maybe he wasn't the same as he'd always been, but Brynn wasn't about to lower her guard. She knew better than to be taken in by a pretty face. Men like Guyer had *trouble* tattooed on their foreheads and *heartbreaker* across their chests.

Okay, not really.

But she'd seen ink on him five years ago. She couldn't recall what tattoos. Undressing such a hot guy wasn't something that happened every day. Okay, it had been a first for her. She hadn't known whether to be stunned or intrigued. Once he'd opened his mouth the next morning, she'd settled on horrified.

Amelia's hands stopped. "You're tensing up."

Brynn breathed in and then out. "Better?"

"Slightly."

As long as Ry was around, she would be tense. "Sorry."

He went over to talk with Regina Ashe and Ella Norton, two of the top women skiers on the team. Both greeted him with friendly hugs.

Amelia leaned close. "If you're that into Ry-Guy, go and talk to him. He's nice."

Muscles bunched. The stone-hard knots matched Brynn's ramrod spine. "I-I'm not into him."

"The way you're watching his every move suggests otherwise." Amelia gave Brynn another rub and then lifted her hands. "Finished. Remember to ice. And with Ry-Guy, you might want to call dibs, just sayin'."

As Amelia walked away, Brynn's cheeks burned.

Ry was at her side in an instant. "Hey. Are you feeling okay?" He touched her forehead with his hand. "No fever."

"I'm fine. Just..." Embarrassed. "Hot."

His gaze ran the length of her, slowly with approval. "I concur."

Was he complimenting her?

Excitement flashed and quick as a blink disappeared. She didn't want him to say anything nice about her. Spending time with him was ski team business, nothing more. "You're supposed to help me, not aggravate me."

"I am helping you."

He was making no sense. "How?"

"By distracting you from whatever's been on your mind."

"Say what?"

Ry tilted his head. "Have you been thinking about what's troubling you?"

The only thing on her mind had been him. Not…her parents. Her mouth parted.

"See." His face brightened. "Working."

Brynn wasn't convinced about any of this. She didn't trust him. His nice-guy routine could be an act. And that meant one thing.

Races and the pressure aside, this would be the longest week of her life.

Thanks to Ryland Guyer.

At the team meeting the next morning, Ry stood against the far wall. He felt out of place. Yes, he was still a member of the team, listed under the alpine A roster on the website, but he wasn't a competitor. Wearing the lanyard and being labeled an "assistant" left a sour taste in his mouth. Even if the badge was the only way for him to access the areas he needed to be with Brynn.

Next season will be different.

It had to be.

He wasn't ready to retire and occupy that empty office next to his dad's. Someday, yes, but not until after Beijing. A gold medal called to him like a siren's song. He couldn't give up. Not when he could taste victory. He wanted that one more time. That was why he'd been working so hard on his recovery and doing everything he could to be in top shape.

2022.

No matter what Chas had said, three years would go by in a blink.

Ry had no doubt he would make the team next season and be standing on the podium again. Even if the alternative might have flashed into his mind a time or two, failing to achieve his goals wasn't an option.

Tolliver said something that led Wes to break out in a silly dance.

Everyone laughed.

With a shake of his head, Frederick dismissed the team.

As skiers rose from their chairs, Ry glimpsed Brynn across the room. His gaze met hers. Something flashed. Attraction? Interest? Or wariness? He nearly laughed. It had to be the last one even though she hadn't looked at him with as much dislike as yesterday.

He headed toward her. They'd made plans to meet after the event, but he wanted to see what she was up to now. Ask if she'd slept well. Find out if there was more she wanted to tell him. She, however, didn't glance his way again. Instead, she left with Taylor. "Bolted" might better describe the way she left.

An unexpected heaviness pressed down on his shoulders.

He straightened, not understanding the reaction. Yes, he wanted to speak with Brynn, but it wasn't a big deal he hadn't. She had somewhere to go. So did he.

Ry headed outside. The cold air surrounded him, much cooler than yesterday and what he was used to in Portland, Oregon, his hometown where he'd been doing his rehab. He pulled his beanie lower over his ears.

Time for a coffee. He would grab a cup before staking out a spot where he could see the course.

A chill inched along his spine. One that was only partly because of the winter weather. Watching the men race today would be difficult. He wanted to be on the slopes even if logically it wasn't in the realm of possibility. The old Ry would have blown off the event today to flirt with snow bunnies and hit the hot tub at the condo. But he wasn't that guy. He didn't want to be him. No matter how difficult being a spectator would be, he needed to cheer on his friends racing. That was the right thing to do.

Footsteps sounded behind Ry.

"Wait up." Sam hurried to catch up to him. "Did you see the course?"

"Only from below."

He fell in step with Ry. "And?"

Ry bit back a smile. Sam was the second fastest on the A team in the super combined and eager to beat Chas in this final competition of the year. Ry remembered when he was chasing the top racer. He didn't mind giving a tip or two. "The race will be won on the lower half so push hard there. Watch your line and stay low."

"You sound like Coach."

That heavy feeling from a few minutes ago returned. Ry shook it off. "Then you'd better pay attention. But I'm a skier, not a coach."

Even if he felt like neither at the moment. But he couldn't allow uncertainty to mess with his head and confidence. Soon, he would receive the all-clear sign from his medical team and be on the mountain where he belonged.

"So, what are you doing with Brynn Windham?" Sam asked.

"Trying to help her focus."

"Rumor has it she'll lose her spot."

"Depends on how she finishes the competition."

"She's better than she's been skiing."

"That's what I've heard."

"So nothing's going on with the two of you again?"

Again echoed in Ry's head. He needed to say something. "Nothing ever went on between us."

Sam's forehead creased. "But you said…?"

"I was young and stupid. Blackout drunk. A jerk." That about summed it up. "What I thought happened hadn't even though I said it did."

"No wonder she's been so pissed at you."

"You noticed?"

Sam laughed. "Impossible to miss the daggers being thrown your way for the last five years."

"I hope she and I are beyond that now." At least the daggers seemed to be lessening after spending time together. "I guess we'll see today."

"After I win, we should see if Brynn and her roommate want to join us. Lila is a sweet kid. They can help me celebrate."

"A little cocky."

"I learned from the best." Sam's grin widened. "You."

"Good luck." Ry hoped that cockiness didn't bite Sam the way it had him.

Brynn cheered for her teammates in the men's super combined—a slalom run and a downhill run. Cowbells clanged. She wiggled her toes, a mix of excitement and wanting to stay warm. "Chas is going to win the overall event."

Two blond braids hung out of Lila's hat. Her face glowed despite her breath hanging on the cold air. She clapped her mitten-covered hands. No doubt to keep the blood circulating. "I can't believe the number of spectators who showed up."

"More will be here for the parade, concert, street party, and fireworks. By the weekend, this place will be jam-packed."

The cold made Lila's cheeks pink. "I can't wait."

Neither could Brynn. Nothing beat the electricity during a competition or the camaraderie with her teammates—from the youngest member on the development team to the seasoned medalists on the A team. Other skiers from the US enjoyed competing against national team members.

The cowbell ringing amped up.

Skiing was the only life she knew. The rush of flying down a course, the exhilaration of completing a fast run, the satisfaction of knowing she'd skied her best.

If only...

Brynn wanted her mojo back, to be at the top of her game after a season of improving and to reach the finish line with a competitive time, not struggling to quiet the doubts in her head. If she wasn't on next season's team, she didn't know what she would do. For the first time, the future scared her, a way she wasn't used to feeling.

She bit her lip.

If she didn't make the team, her sponsors wouldn't stick around long if she wasn't competing at big events. A group of teammates rented a place to stay during the off-season. Would she still be welcome or would her spot go to someone new on the team nomination list?

Probably the latter.

Either Jax or Ace would take Brynn in. Support her. Jax had the money to do that. Ace not so much. But both would help her however they could. But they shouldn't have to take care of their younger sister. Brynn wasn't a child. She would have to find a job so she could afford an apartment and to keep training.

She had no other choice because Sully wouldn't let her come home. He'd made it clear she was no longer welcome and packed up her stuff and sent the boxes to Jax. Sully had suggested she legally change her last name from Windham to Morton, her mom's maiden name. The worst part, not that all of it wasn't horrible, was how her mom hadn't spoken up. She'd picked her husband and sons and left Brynn to face the wrath of the man she'd called "Dad" her entire life. In some ways, that hurt as much or more than Sully's behavior.

"Go, Sam, go!" Lila jumped up and down, not hiding how much she wanted him to win.

Oh, to be young again. Though Brynn would pass on the unrequited love. She read the scoreboard.

"He's doing well."

Sam crossed the finish line and threw his hands in the air.

"Good run," Brynn said.

Lila's grin spread across her face. "He's the best."

One of the best, at least.

Brynn didn't know if she would include Ry in that group. She wondered if he was watching the race. None of her business. Probably best to forget about him while she could because he'd texted her about meeting after the race to prepare for tomorrow. Her emotions over spending more time with him kept flip-flopping from can't-wait-to-see-him to why-do-we-have-to-get-together. She didn't understand why.

This morning when she'd seen him at the team meeting, something in her stomach fluttered. A stupid reaction as if sparks—or anything—could travel across a room. Chalking the response up to hypersensitivity, she hadn't stuck around to speak with him but left to have coffee with Taylor.

That didn't stop Brynn from searching the sea of faces now, but she didn't see Ry. He'd competed with most of these guys for years, some since they were kids, so he would likely be here somewhere.

Unless watching was too rough on him.

Not being able to race must be difficult even though he would be on skis in time for next season. An impressive feat, given the severity of the injuries—from broken bones to internal bleeding—he'd suffered. At one point, he'd been in critical condition. The entire team had been talking about it, hoping and praying for Ry. Even though the past had colored her views of him, she respected how far he'd come since his crash.

She didn't know him well. Calling him a teammate was pushing it, but he seemed to understand her.

I'm helping you. By distracting you from whatever's been on your mind.

Yes, he was doing that.

Thoughts of him had locked themselves front and center in her mind. That bothered her. The last thing she needed was another crush on Ry-Guy.

Not that she had one now.

Or would.

He'd changed, but so had she. Brynn wasn't the same shy girl she'd once been. All she needed to do was focus on her race tomorrow.

Staring up the mountain, she imagined her slalom and downhill tomorrow. Her skis gliding over the snow. Her edges carving turns.

Anticipation buzzed through her.

For the first time in weeks, she couldn't wait to be out on the course.

A good sign. An even better feeling.

Lila sucked in a breath. "That guy's flying."

His split time was faster than Sam's. Not surprising given the skier, a local, was going all out and taking risks.

The crowd erupted into cheers and cowbells clanged when he crossed the finish line.

"No way. He beat Sam's time." Disappointment laced Lila's words.

"The kid will be on the podium," Brynn said. "He nailed the lower half. The course is in great shape."

"Don't expect the same conditions tomorrow. Snowfall will slow the course and cause obstacles." Coach Frederick appeared as if materializing in the crowd with a flick of a wand, or in his case, a tablet. "Visibility may be poor. Be on the lookout for ruts. Rolls may surprise you."

Brynn felt the urge to join the group of racing fans behind them, but she held her ground.

"Be ready for whatever Mother Nature brings," he added.

"Yes, sir." Lila raised her arm as if to salute but then lowered her hand. Coach had that effect on newer skiers. Some older ones, too.

His gaze narrowed on Brynn. "Did you talk to Guyer?"

She looked a little like her mom. That was what everyone had told her. Couldn't Coach Frederick see the resemblance? "Spent time with him yesterday."

"Today?"

"Not yet."

Her tongue felt ten sizes too big for her mouth, swollen as if she were having an allergic reaction. Coach treated her the same as the other members of the team. Would that change if he found out she was his daughter?

For all she knew, he wouldn't care. Sully hadn't.

Was the chance of having a relationship with Frederick beyond athlete-coach worth destroying her family? Especially when she was no longer considered one of them?

The questions plagued Brynn, kept her awake at night, gave her bad dreams, distracted her when her mind should be focused on nothing but skiing.

A vise tightened around her heart.

Best to keep quiet. What else could she do?

"Listen to what Ry has to say," Coach said.

Brynn nodded like a seven-year-old, wanting to please Frederick. She'd been that age when she'd made her first assist on a goal, slid into the boards, and split open her chin. Instead of giving praise, Sully had screamed at her for needing to leave the game to get stitches. She was grown up now, but she still wanted a father...a dad.

"See you two at dinner." With that, Coach left.

She watched him go, trying to see any similarities between the two of them. She might look more like her mother, but Brynn skied like Coach. Well, based on old clips she'd found on the internet, she did.

Wishful thinking, maybe?

Frederick had no children—well, other than her—that she knew about. One rumor floating around suggested he and Coach Tolliver were into each other, but Brynn had never seen anything. But one thing was clear—he wasn't a family guy. Skiing meant everything to him.

"Does he ever seem less intimidating?" Lila whispered.

"Let's just say Wes has always been more approachable." Brynn's excitement for tomorrow's races disappeared. A rock settled at the bottom of her stomach. Typical reaction whenever she was around Coach, except today he hadn't been on her mind. Not until seeing him just now. That was unusual.

Maybe Ry was right that distracting her was a good thing. She'd been thinking about him so much there wasn't room in her brain for anything else, including her birth father.

Could a fix be that simple?

She hoped so. Except she'd rather find another guy to distract her. One whom she didn't have a past with—even if that past was only one night.

"I like talking to Wes. He's nice," Lila said.

Brynn focused on her roommate.

"Wes is great. Tolliver may be our coach, but she's a protégé of Frederick's. You won't find a better alpine coach than him." Saying that filled Brynn with an unfamiliar sense of pride. "Look at Regina's success this season. Or how much Taylor accomplished before her knee injury."

"We're as fast as they are."

"Great attitude. Anything can happen. Like that

local skier placing third."

"Sam got bumped to fourth." Lila sounded so sad.

Lila's crush reminded Brynn of her old one on Ry. Five years had been a lifetime ago. She was older now. One level away from her dream of making the A team and her world was falling apart. Did that mean she hadn't gotten wiser with age? Appeared so, because she wanted to return to December and redo her races since then.

Lila glanced around. "I wonder if he's upset."

"You really like Sam."

"Yes, but…" Lila's frustrated sigh was one Brynn knew well. "He called me kiddo at the team meeting this morning. Not a good sign."

"You're nineteen. He's twenty-seven."

"I'll be twenty next month." Lila placed her hands on her hips and flipped the blond hair sticking out from the bottom of her beanie. "Do I look like a kid?"

"No." She looked like a beautiful actress on a cable channel drama. "But he is older than you and been on the team for years."

"Like Ry." Straightening her hat, Lila smirked. "He's heading toward us, watching you the way he did at this morning's meeting. I'm sure he's got a thing for you. Is the feeling mutual?"

"No 'thing.' No feelings. For either one of us." Brynn didn't need rumors about her and Ry-Guy going around. Been there, done that. She didn't want a repeat. "You heard what Frederick said during the meeting. Ry's working as a team assistant."

Lila sighed. "You're so lucky he's assisting you."

"Lucky? Right, I should buy a lottery ticket," Brynn muttered under her breath.

"He's hot."

Few men were as handsome as Ryland Guyer. A good thing Brynn was immune to his charms. But maybe a booster shot was in order. "There's more to a man than his looks."

"I'm only nineteen, remember?" Lila joked.

Brynn laughed.

Ry zigzagged around people until he reached her and Lila. "Enjoying yourselves, ladies?"

"Today has been fun." Lila beamed. "But I'd rather be racing."

Ry flashed a dazzling, toothpaste-ad-worthy smile. "Tomorrow is your turn to shine. Both of you."

Brynn nodded. The past couple of months she'd felt like a burned-out bulb. Shining would be a welcome change.

"Have plans for this afternoon?" he asked her.

Lila pushed Brynn forward. "She doesn't. But I do. Big plans. Huge ones. In fact, I'd better go. See you two around."

The young skier disappeared into the crowd.

"Those must be some big plans," Ry said.

She would have to make sure Lila understood the

definition of subtlety. "Huge ones."

He laughed. "It's time to talk about the super combined."

"I hope this will be more fun than reviewing video and getting a go-get-em pep-talk à la Tolliver."

"You want fun?" Ry's lips curved into a crooked grin. "I'm the definition of fun."

"As long as your definition includes being fully dressed, I'm game."

"Five years ago… Who am I kidding? Even two, things might have been different, but fully clothed is standard operating procedure these days."

The humor in his voice brought a smile. Brynn wished he didn't have that effect on her, but there was no reason to keep fixating on the past. She would play along for now. "I'll warn you. My expectations are high. I not only want to have fun, but I also want to win."

His grin crinkled the corners of his eyes and stole her breath away.

So not the reaction Brynn wanted to have. She swallowed.

"Let's see what we can do to make that happen," he said.

Ry sounded so confident. A part of her was envious. She used to be confident until the secrets and worries bogged her down. Maybe some of his self-assurance would rub off on her. Standing on the podium might not be a pie-in-the-sky dream.

Brynn pictured herself up there. One of the top three. Maybe number one. Tingles formed in her stomach.

"Ready?" he asked.

Was she?

Ry seemed...different. But his changing didn't matter. It couldn't.

She cared only about saving her spot on the team. Brynn still didn't trust him, but she appreciated his help. Something told her she needed it.

She straightened. "I'm ready."

Chapter Five

Having fun and winning were two of Ry's favorite things even though there'd been less of one and none of the other for over two years. He couldn't wait for the latter to change because he missed the exhilaration and sense of accomplishment standing on the podium brought. Winning filled the empty space inside him in a way nothing else did.

As he reached the street, he waited with Brynn at his side for a car to drive past. They crossed the road.

Her new attitude pleased him. She was smiling and hadn't slammed him once. If anything, she seemed to enjoy herself.

Brynn could be humoring him, but if her slalom and downhill events went well, he didn't care. She needed to get rid of the monkey clinging to her back and wreaking havoc on her skiing. If only she would tell him what was going on inside her head. But since she hadn't, Ry would do what he could.

"What did you think about the race today?" he asked.

"The course was faster than I thought it would be. The water they sprayed froze perfectly. Slick, smooth, and fast. No snow glare, either. Perfect lighting."

Wisps of hair stuck out of her hat. The cold air turned the tip of her nose and cheeks pink. She appeared happy and carefree. More relaxed than when he'd met her in the cafeteria yesterday. He hoped that continued.

"Coach Frederick said the weather wouldn't be as good tomorrow," she added.

"Snow's predicted."

"It won't be the first time." She waved to someone across the street who called her name. "The line the third-place skier took was risky but paid off. I want to study his run. He's from the area. Not quite home field advantage, but he made the most of knowing the hill."

"You sound like a coach." Ry almost laughed, given Sam had mentioned something similar to him earlier.

"Family occupation." She shoved her hands into her coat pockets. "My, um, father coaches in the American Hockey League. My five older brothers followed in his footsteps. Two play professionally. My three oldest brothers coach or work in the front office."

"Did you say five brothers?"

She nodded. "I'm the youngest."

Ry had no idea. "I'm glad one of them didn't beat me up five years ago."

"If I'd told them what happened, you wouldn't have the nose you do today. One is a defenseman in the NHL. It wouldn't have been pretty."

"I wouldn't be the face of Guyer Gear."

"No, but if there was Guyer Garbage…"

"Cute."

"You wouldn't be any longer." She didn't sound like she was joking.

Still, he grinned. "So you think I'm cute?"

"I never said that."

"Not exactly." The way she avoided his gaze told him she did think he was cute. Spending time with Brynn Windham was more fun than he imagined it would be. He wouldn't call her a girly-girl, but she wasn't a tomboy, either. With so many brothers… Something clicked in his brain. "Windham. Jax Windham is your brother?"

"One of them."

The guy was an All-Star, huge and intimidating on the ice. He could have beat Ry without much effort. "Thanks for not saying anything to him or the others."

"Well, I considered telling Jax and Ace on more than one occasion. Ace is the other hockey player. They're the two who are closest to me in age and are overprotective of their baby sister."

"Relieved you took the high road." Ry touched his nose, grateful one of her brothers hadn't rearranged his face. Not that he'd touched Brynn, but his words had harmed her. "So, hockey is big in your family?"

"Hockey is the meaning of life when you're a Windham."

Her dead-serious tone surprised him. "Does everyone ski, too?"

"Only me and my mom. I did better skiing downhill than skating across the ice, so she put me in lessons."

"You must take after her, not your dad."

Brynn stumbled. Her hands flew out of her pockets.

Ry grabbed her to keep her upright. "You okay?"

She licked her lips. "Yes."

He stood there as if frozen in place, arms around her waist, his face inches from hers. The only sound was their breaths, the condensation hanging in the cool air. He loosened his grip as soon as he realized she was steady, but he wasn't in any hurry to put distance between them. Weird, given he wasn't interested in dating.

Finally, she stepped away from him. "Thanks."

Her cheeks reddened, and her smile disappeared. He didn't like the expression on her face—a mixture of surprise, embarrassment, and wariness. In the past, he would have kissed her, but he doubted Brynn would be stunned into smiling. He would try humor instead. "Those snow snakes will trip you every time."

Her mouth curved upward. "Gotta watch your steps. They appear out of nowhere."

Okay, that was better. Not a full smile but close enough. "Is your family coming to watch you race?"

Brynn's shoulders sagged, only slightly but enough he noticed. She retied the scarf around her neck. "No. It's hockey season."

That had to be tough. His parents never missed his stateside races. They attended as many international ones as they could, too. "Your family must be proud of you being on the national team."

She perked up. "My mom is thrilled. Competing at this level was a dream of hers. Ace and Jax come to races when they can. The others… Well, they wish I'd kept playing hockey instead."

Few reached the level where Brynn competed, but her resigned tone bothered him. A family should encourage each other, no matter what sport or hobby one did. "If it's any consolation, my dad supports my comeback, but he didn't always. He still can't wait until I leave competitive skiing behind and work for him."

"Doesn't sound like too bad a gig with a private jet at your disposal. Beats the alternatives."

"What are those?"

"Unemployed and homeless." If she was trying to be funny, the joke fell flat.

He'd never thought about his future that way. Was that what she was worried about happening to her if she lost her spot on the team?

She continued to fiddle with her scarf.

Probably, or she wouldn't have said that. Man, he couldn't imagine having that weighing over him while trying to compete, but she made him realize there were worse things that could happen to him than taking over a successful company. "You're right."

The condo's hallway was empty. People must be skiing or in the hot tub. He wouldn't mind doing the latter with Brynn in a sexy bikini, sitting in the steaming water, her skin and the ends of her hair wet.

Whoa. Where had that come from? That wasn't why he was spending time with Brynn, except…

As long as your definition includes being fully dressed, I'm game.

A swimsuit counted as clothes, right?

Weak, Guyer.

And it was. So was using the excuse the hot water might be good for her hip and loosen her tight muscles.

Guilt coated his throat. He needed to stay focused. Better not even mention hot-tubbing.

He unlocked and opened the door. "After you."

She went in, stopped at the entrance to the galley-style kitchen, and motioned to the items he'd left on the counter. "You cook?"

Her disbelief amused him. "Tonight I'll be baking, but I have many hidden talents."

Brynn raised a questioning brow.

Oops. She might take what he said the wrong way given their—well, his—past. A good thing he hadn't brought up the hot tub.

"Cooking, baking, barbecuing," he clarified. "Not to mention laundry. Forget ironing. A few wrinkles don't bother me."

She studied him as if he were a rare museum exhibit behind glass. "I figured you had someone who did those things for you."

"When I was growing up I did, but not now. I'll be honest, I miss the team's chef. Never ate that well or healthy in my life though he still sends me a menu plan." Ry preheated the oven. He glanced Brynn's way. "What?"

Lines formed above the bridge of her nose. "I'm not used to this."

"A guy who can take care of himself isn't shocking."

"You've never met my brothers."

That made him laugh. He grabbed the bag of chocolate chips. "Picked up a few things to make cookies. My one vice."

She eyed him warily. "I seem to remember a few more."

"In the past."

"We're supposed to watch what we eat, but homemade cookies aren't what I'd call a vice." She removed her coat. "Now the dough is another story. That is the tastiest part."

"No dough tonight." He tossed his coat on a barstool. "Can't have you sick before a race."

She frowned. "Do you know anyone who's gotten sick on cookie dough?"

"No, but it's not happening on my watch."

Her lower lip shifted forward in an adorable pout, a move she had down. "So much for you claiming to be the definition of fun."

"Salmonella is the antithesis of fun," he countered, half joking. "After the giant slalom on Sunday, you can eat as much cookie dough as you want, deal?"

She tilted her head as if thinking about what he'd said. "Deal."

"You can have two cookies tonight. Don't want Coach Tolliver mad at me for feeding you junk food before a big race." Ry wrapped the bag of frozen peas in a kitchen towel before handing it to her. "Ice your hip while I get started. You can sit on a barstool or the couch. Whichever is more comfortable."

"Barstool." She sat at the breakfast bar. "I want to watch you."

"Me baking is that surprising?"

"Yes, but in a good way."

"Wait." He stopped, thought about what she'd said, and grinned. "Did you say something nice about me?"

"Maybe."

"I must not be a total cad, then."

"I'm willing to give you the benefit of the doubt for now." Her lighthearted tone told him she was teasing. "I'll make my final decision after I see the cookies."

"You won't be disappointed."

"I hope not."

Awareness pulsed between them, strong and undeniable. The connection felt real, almost electric, and pulled him in.

She tilted her head, exposing her neck. All he could think about was leaving a trail of kisses from her collar to her lips.

Moisture filled Ry's mouth. His pulse accelerated. The temperature in the condo rose twenty degrees. He took a step toward her, wanting to get closer, but then stopped.

This can't happen.

His recovery, training, Beijing.

He went around the breakfast bar and gathered

the ingredients in the kitchen. The distance didn't stop him from breathing in her scent—something citrusy. Every nerve ending twitched, conscious of Brynn, the rise and fall of her chest with each breath, her adjusting the ice pack against her hip.

Yes, she was pretty.

Hot, actually.

But her appearance shouldn't matter.

He was used to being around gorgeous models—holding them, touching them, kissing them. All for the camera.

But this sudden connection with Brynn?

The low ache might be familiar, but the longing in his chest wasn't.

It had to stop.

He didn't want a date or anything else with a woman—any woman. But as Chas had mentioned the other day, *three years until Beijing is a long time.* That must be the reason Ry was feeling…off around her. A long workout might help.

"Are those walnuts on the counter?" Brynn asked.

"Yes." Ry read the recipe on the bag of chocolate chips. "Want nuts in the cookies?"

"Please."

Her face brightened, making him wish he had his cell phone handy to take a photo. He stiffened.

What was wrong with him?

Ry didn't need pictures of her. He was supposed to be protecting himself, keeping his distance from others, not letting them get close and steal what control he did have. As soon as she left, he needed to do a hundred push-ups and sit-ups, take a shower, and refocus on his goal.

2022. Gold.

No distractions allowed.

That included women.

Brynn.

"This week is going to be a bit nuts," she added. "Why not go all in with the cookies?"

This is nuts. Ry swallowed.

Time to put the fun on the back burner and take charge of the situation. Do what needed to be done so he could return to Portland and focus on his rehabilitation and training. He motioned to the tablet sitting on the breakfast bar. "I'll queue up the videos I want you to watch."

The scent of baking cookies filled Ry's condo. Brynn's mouth watered. Two cookies would be plenty for her stomach, but she couldn't get enough of him. An odd reaction given the circumstances, but he was easy on the eyes. That had to be the reason watching Ry bake in the kitchen made her heart beat like she was at the end of a cardio workout. She was happy she'd taken off her jacket. Otherwise she'd be sweating big-time.

Yes, the aesthetic of Ryland Guyer explained

everything.

Including why her gaze was glued on him as he bent over, checking the cookies in the oven. His jeans fit to a T, suggesting whatever muscle mass and weight he'd lost after his crash had returned better than ever. That wasn't all. His biceps showed beneath the stretched fabric of his long-sleeved Henley. He'd been lifting weights, not only using the different colored TheraBands hanging on a nearby doorknob for physical therapy exercises.

"Golden brown." His gaze slid to hers. A sly expression crossed his face. "Something catch your attention?"

Busted. Heat rushed to her face.

Ry's smile reached his eyes, making him handsomer if that were possible.

Eye candy. That was all. She bit her lip.

His brows drew together, and he straightened. "Something wrong?"

"No." The video had finished playing. Brynn didn't remember what she'd been watching, but she needed to say something other than *nice butt*. "I, um, need a new bag of peas."

He removed another from the freezer, wrapped it in a towel, and handed her the bundle. The way he'd been doing since she arrived. Twenty minutes on, twenty minutes off.

"What goals are you shooting for?" he asked.

"Staying on the team. Everything builds on that

happening."

"What about long-term?"

"I had them." A plan on how to make it happen, too. "Before things…fell apart. Now I can't see past the team nominations being announced. That will decide what I need to focus on over the summer and later."

"No matter what happens in May, you need a bigger goal even if it seems like a reach. Everything I've been doing gets me closer to mine."

Whatever his ways, Ry sounded confident. She leaned over the breakfast bar. "What's that?"

"Beijing."

"Big goal." But she wasn't surprised because he'd rambled on about winning the gold medal when he'd been drunk five years ago. Something about how silver and bronze wouldn't do. Had to be gold. "How do you plan to get there?"

The oven timer rang. He removed the cookie tray. "I have a list of steps I need to take. That keeps me focused on what I need to do."

Lists and steps sounded more methodical than she would have expected from someone so casual and carefree. Or maybe he *had* changed and wasn't like that anymore. "What kind of steps?"

"Take my getting on skis again. First I needed to be able to use a walker, crutches, stand on my own, walk, jog, and then run. Those are the steps I've accomplished. I still have more on my list."

"Sounds complicated."

"Not if you write it down. I made lists and keep them on my phone so I know where I am at all times," he explained. "I know everything I need to do from conditioning to lifestyle changes."

"Lifestyle?"

"No more partying, late nights, alcohol, or women."

He'd mentioned his drinking and not having the same vices as before. Nothing she'd seen these past two days suggested otherwise. Maybe party boy Ryland Guyer had grown up. "You made steps for those, too?"

"More of a what-not-to-do list." His face flushed. "It was time."

His tone was light, but his gaze was serious.

"You have plenty of time to be ready for 2022." The way he'd turned himself around impressed her. He could have kept on the same path, injured not only himself, but also hurt others. Except he'd stopped. Made changes. Was working toward a big goal. Maybe the coaches hadn't been crazy. Maybe she could learn something from Ryland Guyer. "I used to dream about winning a gold medal, but now that seems…impossible."

"Where you are now isn't where you'll be forever."

"I sure hope not."

He laughed. "Talk to me about bobbling at the bottom of the course."

She'd been sneaking peeks at him, not studying the video. "Let me watch it again."

Brynn hit the reload button. No one except Mom took care of her like this. Jax tried, but he was more of a buy-something-to-make-her-feel-better kind of guy. Ace would offer a hand, when he thought he might get the phone number of one of her friends. Her three older brothers might bring her a glass of water if they happened to be visiting the house, but setting the timer to know when to put on and take off ice packs?

No way.

She'd never been serious enough with any guys she dated to ask for their help. This was a new experience, one she kind of liked.

"Before we start, do you need anything else?" Ry asked.

The last time someone had done so much for her was when she'd had her wisdom teeth pulled the day after her seventeenth birthday. Her mom had made sure Brynn was comfortable. Jax had made a special trip home with ice cream and straws. Ace had skipped classes at college to bring her candy she couldn't eat and a pop music magazine she used to read when she was twelve. Both had joked and teased her about having chipmunk cheeks. As usual, her other brothers hadn't called. Sully, who had been out of town, hadn't, either.

Ry's attention made Brynn feel as if someone cared. Someone who wasn't a member of her family.

The hair on the back of her neck rose. She hadn't forgotten what he'd done in the past. He might have an ulterior motive. She had to be careful, keep her guard up. What was the adage?

Fool me once, shame on you. Fool me twice, shame on me.

"Thanks, but I'm good." Brynn focused on the video. This time, she recognized the course where her season fell apart—Are in Sweden.

"What happened?" he asked, no judgment in his voice.

Still her stomach clenched. A good thing she hadn't tried a cookie because she was nauseous. A chill grabbed hold of her. Brynn wrapped her arms around her waist.

"I hit a rut and couldn't recover." She didn't need to watch the clip again. Not when she was reliving it. "I got distracted."

One miniscule lapse was all it took in races won and lost by hundredths of a second.

"What distracted you?"

Ry wasn't trying to pry, but she had to be careful.

"Personal stuff." That seemed safe and vague enough to say. "We're supposed to tune everything out when we're racing, and I've never had a problem doing that before, but I couldn't then and paid the price. I was lucky I didn't hurt myself."

There. She'd told him more than anyone else. She hoped that was enough.

"That wasn't the only time," he said finally.

She dragged her teeth over her lip. "No."

But it had to be the last, or she would lose…everything.

Chapter Six

Sitting on a barstool, Brynn fought the urge to spin around so she wasn't facing Ry. She didn't want to talk about this. If the identity of her birth father came out publicly, she wouldn't be the only one affected. But she was feeling closer to Ry. Something she didn't understand compelled her to tell him...more.

Brynn struggled to figure out what to say. "My parents. They distracted me."

That much was nonspecific, but included the involved parties. She wasn't the first athlete to have parent issues though she'd never heard of *this* situation.

"I didn't know they were at Lake Louise," he said.

"They weren't, but after the competition, we…argued. Over the phone."

As Ry scratched his head, a puzzled expression formed on his face. "That was in December. It's March."

"Yeah." The conversation with Sully, the man she'd called Dad for twenty-four years, had been playing on a continuous loop for months, ripping apart her confidence and her heart.

The podium was yours, Brynn, but you screwed up. Just like you always do.

I was trying to cut time, go for the win.

You don't know what winning means. You're weak. A loser. You've never been one of us.

But, Dad—

Don't call me that. I'm done pretending to be your father. You're a disgrace to the Windham name, when you aren't even one. Your mother should have gotten rid of you when she had the chance.

Brynn wanted to cover her ears now the way she had then, but nothing quieted the harsh words and hateful tone, not even skiing. She wanted to forget what Sully had said, pretend nothing had changed, but his words echoed through her head, continuously playing, during races and when she tried to sleep.

"Still not over it." She tried to limit the emotion she showed.

Her mother had begged Brynn to keep quiet, so she had. Brynn didn't want to be the one to tear the family apart, but that left her stuck in limbo, unable to take action or move on or get the help she needed to handle this.

Brynn rubbed her arms. She had never felt so lonely.

Ry walked around the breakfast bar. He handed her a cookie. "This might help."

She had to smile. Whatever she might have thought of Ry-Guy, today's version was warm and strong and came bearing sweets at the perfect time. Her stomach hadn't totally settled, but she took a bite.

Not bad.

He moved his jacket from the other stool and sat.

Brynn finished the cookie. "Thanks. Better than I expected."

"I have another with your name on it."

A speck of flour was on his shirtsleeve. She brushed it off. The right thing to do. Not because she wanted to touch him.

His breath hitched, and he blinked twice.

The microwave timer buzzed, breaking whatever spell had been between them. She removed the ice pack from her hip.

"Have you tried resolving things with your parents?" he asked.

A lump in her throat formed, burned.

Sully hadn't ever wanted her. Growing up, he'd

barely tolerated her. She saw that now. He also never wanted to see her again. Her mother claimed that had been emotion talking, but Brynn knew better.

Thank goodness she'd been racing in Europe over Christmas or she would have been on her own. The way she would be when the season ended. Normally she would head home for a short break before training began again, but she was no longer welcome there.

Would Coach Frederick want to know he had a daughter? What if he found out about her and didn't care? An adult daughter might not fit into his single lifestyle. Sully had rejected her. She didn't want Coach to do the same thing.

Ry leaned toward her. "Brynn?"

"I haven't." She forced the response from her on-fire throat.

"Must be tearing you up inside."

A familiar weight pressed against Brynn's chest. She struggled to breathe.

The corners of her eyes stung. Not in front of Ry. Crying would be bad.

She nodded, not trusting her voice, before staring at the ceiling.

As he swiveled his stool in her direction, his leg bumped into hers. The slight contact comforted her, and she yearned for more. A touch or better yet, a hug. She'd felt so alone for the past three months even when she was surrounded by her teammates.

Brynn wanted to reach out to him, open up more, but she couldn't. Not when doubts remained about him. She hadn't exactly been nice to him, either, though she was doing better.

"The next week you were at Val d'Isère," he said.

Another nod. Memories of the tour stop in France flooded her mind. She should have been living the high life competing at a World Cup event. Instead, she was trying to keep her family from imploding.

Ry's gaze held hers. "You were in third place and missed a gate—"

"A random thought at the wrong time." She hadn't skied at the level she should. Not even close. "I was going to the European Cup, but I wanted to show the coaches I had the talent and speed for the A team. The first run went well. I was in the zone the entire time, but then during the next one..." *Loser. You've never been one of us.* Hearing Sully's voice in her head had broken her concentration. "I lost focus. Came up on a turn too late. Missed the gate."

"Same thing happened again."

It wasn't a question. She nodded and then took a breath. "Things fell completely apart during the NorAm races. Which I'm sure you know. And here I am. Pathetic and about to be dropped from the team."

"Not pathetic. What's stuck in your head is messing you up."

"I'm supposed to ski, not think. But I can't." A

91

familiar script from her childhood, one she thought she'd moved on from, played in her head. "I'm unfocused. Weak."

"You're strong. You've kept racing. Trying to overcome whatever happened with your parents." His tender tone seeped into her, filling the empty places inside her with his compassion. He wiped the wetness from her cheek with his fingertips.

Oh, no. Every muscle tensed. She hadn't realized she was crying.

Brynn turned her head.

He held her chin, so she couldn't. "You just need to fix what's going on in your head."

"I've been trying. Nothing's worked."

"Sounds like you need to talk to your parents."

Her heart pounded, each beat reverberating up her neck and centering in her head. A pressure built behind her forehead. She rubbed her temples, but that didn't help.

Hold it together. Don't say anymore.

"Brynn?" he asked.

"I can't," she croaked.

"It might be the only way for you to get over whatever was said."

No, there had to be another way. There would be no mending bridges. Sully had burned theirs. Her mother, desperate to keep Brynn's birth father's identity a secret, remained committed to her husband, saying all Sully needed was time.

But it had been three months. Nothing would change.

What could Brynn do except stay quiet?

Going to Coach wouldn't only mess up things for her family. Talking to him during the championships could turn into a disaster for the team—her friends. Coach might get distracted when he needed to be focused on skiers. Negative publicity would overshadow the races and results. Accusations of favoritism if she got a coach's discretion to stay on the team could discredit Frederick's stellar reputation.

Not worth the risk.

She wouldn't put her needs ahead of her team's. Or her family. "I'll work harder to tune out the noise in my head."

"Can you do that?" Ry asked.

"Probably" wasn't the answer he wanted to hear. "I have no choice. Maybe after…"

The nominations were announced.

If she lost her spot, that would be on her. No one else, including Frederick, would be responsible. And if she were no longer on the team, would his being her birth father matter? She would never see him unless she made the team the next season.

Her muscles bunched tighter.

"Hey." Ry touched her shoulder gently. "You don't have to talk to your mom and dad today. But whatever went down has ruined your season and put your spot on the team in jeopardy. You need help to figure this out. More than I can give you. I know a sports psychologist—"

"No."

"This is what they're trained to do, Brynn. Dr. Dean worked wonders with me. He understands an athlete's mentality. Drive. He was exactly what I needed. He can help you."

Ry made his doctor sound like a wizard. He meant well, but… "My first race is in less than fifteen hours. Unless Dr. Dean uses magic or hypnosis and can see me via Skype, I need to wait."

"You'll talk to him after the championships then?"

The hope in Ry's voice matched the glint in his eyes. Both tugged at her heart. Brynn didn't want to involve another person in this, but Ry was right. Her family situation was interfering with her skiing and messing up her future with the team. She had to do something. "I'll talk to him next week."

"What are you going to do *this* week?"

She pictured her mother and her two youngest brothers. For some strange reason, Ry appeared in the image, too. "I don't know. But there are cookies, and you're here. That's more than I had at my last competition."

Brynn hoped that would be enough.

Ry turned off the tablet. His large hand covered hers.

Her heart bumped.

His skin was warm and rough. Not as smooth as she would have thought given his wealthy upbringing.

He rubbed his thumb against her skin with a gentle back-and-forth motion. "You need more than that."

His presence comforted. His touch soothed. His words made her believe things might be okay. Funny and more than a little disturbing, given this was Ry-Guy, but she wouldn't want to be with anyone else. "Have any ideas?"

"Well, my dad prides himself on being an idea guy," Ry said. "He brainstorms a list of ten items, then crosses off the first five because he says they're too obvious."

"What if one of the first five is the best idea?" Brynn asked.

"I don't know, but remember, this is coming from the guy who's got an empty office next to his, so we can work closely together when I join the company. It's been there since he moved into the corporate headquarters four years ago."

His playful tone told Brynn that Ry cared about his dad, but he preferred skiing. She envied him having a father who wanted to spend time with him that much. "I'd love to work that close to my father."

"I didn't know you liked hockey so much."

Oh, no. She'd said too much. Time to get back on topic.

She shrugged. "I'm not sure I can come up with a

list of ten things."

"Let's come up with a few steps instead. What's the most important thing you want to do tomorrow?"

"Win."

"What do you have to do to win?"

She half laughed. "Finish the race. Both races."

"Good." Excitement gleamed. "What else?"

"Relax."

"By..."

Brynn's gaze traveled to his lips. Wrong answer. Not to mention a bad idea, but she had to say something. "Eating cookies."

"Not what I would have thought of but..." He reached for another cookie. "Knock yourself out."

At the start of the season, she'd been brave, able to say anything to anyone, but now she was afraid to speak—afraid she would say the wrong thing.

She bit into the cookie. She was happy the old Ry-Guy was no longer around, but she hoped the old Brynn wasn't gone forever.

At the team meeting the next morning, Ry listened to Wes's weather report for the women's super combined, consisting of one slalom and one downhill run—the same as the men's yesterday. The current cloudy skies and snow flurries weren't bad, but weather could affect visibility and the course later.

That wouldn't help Brynn, even with the list of steps they'd come up with last night. The weather could be a big problem. That worried him.

She needed to be totally focused. Each error, however small, and the skis setup—from the wax on the bottom and the bevel on the edge—could make the difference between a podium finish and placing in the middle of the standings.

Ry wasn't competing, but he felt amped up, ready to race. A way he hadn't felt in a long time. Not a problem. He'd be on the slopes soon.

The meeting finished, but he remained seated to let the women exit first since they were racing today.

Chas patted his shoulder. "Watching the ladies?"

"Wouldn't miss it."

"So what's the deal with you and Brynn?"

"No deal." Ry didn't want to give anyone the wrong impression. Sure, random thoughts about her that had nothing to do with skiing kept popping into his mind, but he chalked those up to proximity and her attractiveness. Not a problem. Helping her—spending time with her—was completely manageable. "I was asked to help, and I am."

Chas laughed. "Gotta hand it to you, Ry-Guy. You've embraced adversity. Wouldn't go down without a fight. And now you've found a way to stay on Coach's good side without skiing."

"I'm just doing my part for the team." The less Ry said, the better. Today belonged to Brynn and the female members of the US Ski Team.

"Heading to the street party later?" Chas asked.

"Are you and Taylor going?"

"Yes, but Dwyer wants wingmen."

Had Ry been as bad as Jon Dwyer when it came to women? Probably worse.

"I'll have to see." Ry wasn't making plans. If Brynn needed an ear or a shoulder, he wanted to be available. He had no idea how today would go. He hoped she killed it, and they'd be celebrating tonight.

The room cleared.

Coach Frederick sidled up to the table.

Tolliver was beside him. "Brynn appears more relaxed this morning. Is she?"

"Not really," Ry admitted. "But she opened up a little about the stuff going on."

Tolliver smiled. "Good. We need the old Brynn back. I've got to go."

The women's coach left the room.

Frederick stayed. "What did Brynn say?"

"She's having family problems. Something's going on with her mom and dad, but she won't say what."

Ry hoped she would tell him more, but each word last night seemed to cause her pain. He hated seeing her hurting. After she'd left the condo, he'd ordered her a book from Cassandra's Attic, an independent bookstore in San Francisco. He'd met the owner, Cassie McKnight, and her husband, Troy, this month at a wedding between one of her employees, Cara, and movie star Brody Simmons. The book—about using mistakes as steps toward success—wasn't much, but he thought it might help Brynn.

"I haven't met her parents," Coach said. "Just her two brothers. Big, athletic guys."

"Hockey players." Ry touched his straight nose again. "I didn't know one of her brothers is Jax Windham."

"Who?"

"You don't follow hockey."

"No."

"Plays in the NHL. Hockey is her family's life. Her dad coaches and all five of her brothers are involved in the sport."

Coach's brows drew together. "Five older brothers?"

Ry nodded.

"I didn't know that." Coach glanced at his cell phone. "I've got to run."

Distracted, Coach hurried out of the meeting room. Not surprising. His life revolved around the ski team, and he'd be at the bottom of the course as racers finished.

Ry wanted to emulate Coach by being one hundred percent committed to skiing. He had to be to reach his goals. But at the same time, Ry was torn. Something was missing. When he looked to the future, he didn't want the rest of his life to consist of only one thing—working for Guyer Gear. He wanted…balance.

Was that even possible?

Not now. And possibly not later, given how many hours his dad worked.

Would Ry ever feel as if he had control of his life? He hadn't since his crash and everything that followed. Instead, he clung to what he could manage—whom he let into his inner circle and working out.

As Ry rose from the table, he checked his cell phone. He could return to the condo before going to the racecourse.

"Ry."

Brynn's voice made him turn.

She stood in the doorway. Two braids hung out from the bottom of her beanie. Her warm-up pants were tucked into a pair of boots, and she wore a team jacket. The clothes hid her curves, but her face glowed.

Beautiful.

A ball of heat centered in his gut and then spread outward in the shape of a circle until the tendrils reached the top of his head and the tips of his fingers and toes. Her mouth drew his attention, especially the way the bottom lip had a slight pout to it, as if inviting him to take a taste.

Ry wanted to kiss Brynn. Distract her, so nothing about her family was on her mind today.

Yeah, right. That was the only reason he was

thinking about kissing.

He nearly laughed.

Not his best idea if he wanted to show Brynn he'd changed, not reverted to old habits. Bad ones.

"Hey." His voice sounded funny, so he cleared his throat. "The weather predictions were right."

"Fun times ahead with sucky visibility." She peered out the window. "But maybe the snow is what I need to keep my head in the race."

No matter what the conditions, she wouldn't blame her performance on anything other than herself. Ry respected Brynn. Besides ordering the book last night, he'd left a message for Dr. Dean in case she changed her mind and wanted to talk to him sooner.

Not butting in. Being proactive as his mom would say.

"Ready?" Ry asked.

Nodding, Brynn cut the distance between them, her steps purposeful. She stopped an arm's length away. "No matter what happens today, I wanted to thank you. I appreciate your help. I needed it, more than I realized."

Her gratitude made him stand taller. A strange urge compelled him to wrap his arms around her. A hug would be better than kissing her, right?

Not touching her would be safer. "Anytime."

And he meant it. Something about Brynn Windham roused his protective instincts.

"Good." She half laughed. "Because I have three more events after today."

He didn't want to overwhelm her with advice. She had coaches to tell her what to do. "Stay focused."

"And go fast." She inhaled deeply. "I can do this."

"Yes, you can." He pressed his arms against his sides to keep from reaching out to her. The urge to touch her remained strong. He had no idea why, but whatever the cause, he was losing the battle.

A retreat wasn't possible, so Ry gave in. He brushed his lips across her cheek. "For luck. Not that you need it."

She laughed. "I'll take all the luck I can get. Thanks."

"See you afterward?"

"I'd like that very much."

So would he. In fact, he couldn't wait.

A prickle of unease slithered along his spine, but he ignored it. No reason to worry. He was here to help Brynn and the team. Nothing else.

Chapter Seven

Heart pounding, Brynn skied between the red and blue gates marking the downhill course. The adrenaline flowed, and she felt as if she could fly. Nothing beat racing. Just her and the mountain.

She tucked to pick up speed. Flurries fell, but not enough to affect visibility. Gray skies could cause flat light, but that wasn't a problem today. She saw shadows and other things coming up on the course.

Her skis skidded the wrong way, and she felt out of control for a second, but she made it through the turn. Ruts had formed due to the fresh snow.

She nearly sat on her tails. Not on purpose. Corrected her position. Crouched lower. Crossed the finish line.

Spectators cheered, and cowbells clanged.

She'd made it.

Elation rocketed through her. She'd finished the race—both of them—to complete the super combined. Maybe Ry had given her a bit of luck. She hadn't expected a kiss on the cheek, but thinking about his sweet gesture made her smile widen.

She stopped. A rooster's tail of snow flew from her skis.

Breathing hard, Brynn gripped her poles tighter and glanced at the scoreboard.

Her shoulders dropped. Her stomach clenched.

Not fast enough. Mistakes had cost her. She wouldn't be standing on the podium today.

But you finished.

The steps she and Ry had brainstormed last night worked. This was a big accomplishment. Her hands tingled though she wasn't cold. She stood taller as if she'd burned off twenty pounds during the run.

Yes. She'd finally accomplished something by finishing, but who knew if that would be enough to salvage a season of poor results?

People called her name. She waved to the crowd. None of the faces stood out, more like blurs surrounded by bright colors, but her teammates were there. Ry, too.

Brynn exited through the event sponsor's inflatable gate. Coach Frederick was waiting for her. Seeing no frown on his face brought relief, but he wasn't smiling, either. Guess she'd find out what his expression meant.

She was five-eight, but Coach towered over her, more perception than reality. He was an imposing figure in his team jacket and hat. He drew stares wherever he went. Young skiers and eager parents wanted to catch his attention.

Well, she had Frederick's. As her coach, not her dad. She wanted a father to cheer for her, whether she did well or poorly.

Not going to happen.

Knowing that, hurt.

The same as when she'd been younger and wanted Sully to teach her how to ride a bike or watch her race. She might be older, but the yearning was the same now as then.

Deep breaths filled her lungs with cold air. If only she could see Mike Frederick as just a coach, the man who pushed her and her teammates to ski faster and dig deeper to improve, but she kept thinking of him as her father. Hoping he would want her as a daughter. Wondering what had brought him and her mother together at that wedding.

She waited for Coach's barrage of criticism. Something he unleashed on all skiers, not just her. The first time he'd gotten on Brynn, she'd been new on the national scene. Her fat, hot tears had made Coach's face redder. She'd wanted to die, take up snowboarding. Until she'd realized he was correct. Her skiing weaknesses reflected her personality weaknesses. She'd worked hard to fix that and had. Only now she was back where she'd been. So not good.

"You went for it," Coach said.

Brynn lifted her goggles up on her helmet. "Had nothing to lose."

"Almost lost it when you went back on your tails."

Nothing missed his eagle eyes, but Brynn had given her all during the race. She raised her chin. "But I didn't. Just couldn't make up the time."

Coach started to speak but stopped. He tried again. "Better than not finishing."

Brynn nodded. Nerves knocked like skis against a bumpy course. She didn't know if finishing a run would be enough to keep her spot. She doubted it.

"Tomorrow's another race." Coach sounded encouraging, and she bit her lip at the small sign of hope. He touched her shoulder with a gloved hand. "Lila's coming up soon."

Dismissed. He had other skiers to watch.

Good. Putting distance between them would release the tension that had built up.

Being around Mike Frederick made Brynn nervous. What should be a normal interaction between coach and athlete became a near panic attack. She was afraid to talk to him, scared she might say something wrong and raise his suspicions, or worse, blurt the truth so she could move on. But that would ruin, well, everything for her mom and brothers. The fears made every conversation stressful and intense, whether during a practice or a race.

Sam yelled, "Good job."

Jon flashed her a thumbs-up. Others shouted. All were smiling.

Grateful for their support, she raised a pole and struck a pose. Each teammate knew her struggles this season. They'd tried to help even though she'd kept the reason for her poor performance a secret. She didn't want who her birth father was to change anything. Not her position on the team or how anyone viewed her or Coach Frederick. Skiing had been her escape from Sully's disappointment in her. Now Brynn's place of refuge had been overrun with her soap opera life. She didn't want the identity of her father to hurt the team.

Chas stood behind Taylor with his arms around her. The two were the perfect couple and made for each other. Both physically and emotionally. They supported each other one hundred percent, on good days but especially on bad ones. That was what Brynn wanted to find someday.

Knee surgery kept Taylor from competing, but Chas had been at her side the entire time. Even though she wasn't racing today, she seemed content and happy with her life.

Taylor had accepted her injury and that she might never ski at the same level or compete again.

Brynn didn't understand how her friend and teammate had done that. Was it because of Chas? Or something inside Taylor?

Imagining a life without being on the team, the one bright spot in Brynn's world, made her sick to her stomach. This was where she belonged. She didn't want to lose that and her teammates.

Think positively.

Focus on the steps.

Snowflakes twirled and danced on their way to the ground, oblivious of the skiers and spectators, who wished they'd go away.

Skis off, she watched the course to see the next competitor. Her time was faster than Brynn's. Not surprising, but that meant she would be knocked down another spot.

Tomorrow's another race.

Coach's words brought comfort and hope. It was the first time since December she'd felt that way.

Progress?

About time.

Keeping her mother's secret was destroying everything Brynn had worked to achieve, but she believed something good had to come of this. At least for her family.

Ry came toward her, weaving his way through the crowd with confidence. The ends of his hair poked from underneath his red beanie. His sky-blue eyes contrasted to the gray clouds.

Seeing him made her feel lighter, as if everything might be okay. She'd needed a glimmer of hope to hold onto during this dark time. Funny how he'd been the one to give her that.

"Hi." He wrapped his arms around her and lifted her off the ground.

She inhaled sharply, a combination of surprise and her nerve endings springing to life from being so close to him. He was warm and smelled delicious—a hint of hot cocoa and male, an addictive combination.

"You skied well," he said.

"Thanks, but I wish I would have been faster."

"You were fast and focused." Ry squeezed her tighter before placing her on the ground. "You got over the mental hang-up today."

"You helped me."

"A list may have helped you prepare ahead of time, but you did this, Brynn." Something like pride flashed across his face. "You."

The noises from the spectators continued, but the sound seemed to be muted. People brushed past, but they quickly faded into the background.

Her legs wobbled as if she'd ridden her bike up a mountain. She opened her mouth to talk, but her tongue seemed twisted and too big. Her senses felt heightened.

All because of Ry.

His warm breath caressed her neck, heating her insides and giving her chills on the outside. She shouldn't, but she leaned against him. Being closer to him felt…right.

"You finished both races," he continued. "That's a win in my book."

In his arms, she might as well be standing in first place. His lips were only inches away. Close enough for a kiss.

"We'll work on the physical part next," he said without missing a beat.

Anticipation surged. Physical with him sounded perfect. Except he meant skiing. She shouldn't be disappointed.

Focus, Brynn.

She did. "Which part?"

His gaze held hers. "All of them. I'm here for you. I'll make sure it all comes together."

She wanted to kiss him.

Her heart slammed against her ribs.

She couldn't, could she?

Pros and cons battled inside her brain.

Yes, no, maybe. Her teammates were standing around somewhere. Coaches and staff, too. If this were another time and place…

But she was here to race. Win. She didn't need more distractions, let alone complications. A kiss could be a big complication.

Or a kiss could be simple, no big deal.

Make it fast.

That sounded good to her.

Brynn brushed her lips across his. A simple kiss. A short one. No big deal.

"Thank you." She expected him to let go of her. He didn't. "What if someone is watching us?"

"Everyone is staring at the course." Ry pulled her closer and covered her mouth with his.

Oh, wow. Wow, wow, wow.

His lips moved over hers. So warm. So tasty.

She melted into Ry, wrapping her arms around him. His jacket kept her from getting too close, but his lips against hers were more than enough. His kiss heated her blood better than a sip of a peppermint schnapps-spiked hot chocolate after a day on the slopes. Sensations shot through her, loosening her muscles better than après ski hot-tubbing.

His hand ran up and down her back.

More. She wanted more kisses, more of him.

She parted her lips, deepened the kiss.

Ry went with her, pressing against her mouth. His hunger made her feel desired and special.

Her control slipped. Her heart pounded.

Stopping the kiss was the logical thing to do. Except…

His kiss changed. Slowed. Softened.

He moved away, stared at her with awe—exactly

how she was feeling, as if she'd skied another race and won. Her lips tingled. She wanted another kiss. *Lots* more.

Ry's kiss hadn't been simple or no big deal. His kiss had knocked her world into another galaxy. One that lacked oxygen, made her struggle to take a breath.

The corners of his mouth lifted. His playful—dare she say suggestive—grin made her pulse skyrocket again.

He winked. "Not the physical parts I was talking about, but it's a good start."

Her muscles twitched. She doubted that was from the lactic acid built up during the race. A nervous laugh escaped. "I'm not sure what to say."

"Tell me what you're thinking."

"You kiss better sober than drunk." As soon as she spoke, she regretted it.

He laughed. "I'm glad you liked this one better, since I don't remember the first one."

"Much better. That worries me."

His brows furrowed. "Why?"

Cowbells and cheers erupted as if she'd hit the unmute button. She took two steps back. As Ry had said, people were staring at the course, not at them. That brought no relief.

Her fingers and toes felt numb. She couldn't catch her breath.

Brynn worried kissing him had been a mistake. That what little control she'd found to finish these two races would be lost now, and she'd be in a worse place than where she started.

"This was, um, nice, but I'm sorry." The words rushed out, one on top of the other. "I got caught up in the moment. I can't afford to lose focus again."

A vein pulsed at his jaw until a smile spread across his face. "The kiss was not nice. It was hot, but you don't have to worry. I've sworn off women, remember?"

He'd mentioned that, but... "Then why did you kiss me?"

"We were celebrating your run. That's how we do it on the A team."

She wasn't sure if he was joking or not. "I've never heard that."

"Our version of a secret handshake. Only with lips." He kept a straight face, but unmistakable mischief gleamed. "You should see what we do when one of us wins."

Self-preservation tamped down her curiosity. He had to be teasing. "I'll take your word for it."

"Win tomorrow and find out for yourself."

Temptation flared like a Roman candle on the Fourth of July. Brynn wasn't one to walk away from a challenge, but her lips throbbed from his kiss, and this was Ry-Guy.

Yes, he'd helped her succeed today, but her trust in him wavered like the flags on the top of a course. Who knew what he was up to? No one could change that much, could they?

Brynn wasn't sure she wanted to know the answer.

She stood taller. "I want to win, and if I do, I want something better than seeing how the A team celebrates."

"Tell me what would you like, and I'll make it happen."

He was saying the right things, but she wasn't sure if that was enough.

"I don't know yet." She tilted her chin. "But chocolate should be involved. Maybe cookies."

And definitely more kisses.

Except she wasn't ready to say that aloud. Not yet.

Chapter Eight

That evening, the street party was in full swing in front of a local bar and grill. Ry stood on the edge of the crowd. Sam was going on about his favorite subject—women. Jon Dwyer had deserted them for a pair of blond snow bunnies. Chas and Taylor had been holding hands, whispering, before disappearing into a restaurant.

Ry half listened to Sam over the music playing. He was more interested in staring at Brynn, fifteen feet away, with Lila and a male skier he didn't recognize.

He should pay attention to Sam, but the sight of Brynn in her faded jeans, boots, and hooded white parka snared Ry's gaze like a steel trap. *So beautiful.* Sweet and sexy like her kiss.

Her kissing him had caught him off guard earlier. Unexpected, but not unwelcome. Far from it. All he'd wanted were more kisses, completely forgetting about his so-called lifestyle changes, at least where women were concerned.

For a nanosecond, he'd understood what Chas had meant. A minivan with a ski rack on top didn't seem so bad, but the image implied settling down, a stable life, working for Guyer Gear.

Not happening.

Instead, he pictured himself with Brynn, lips against each other, and preferred that image. More kissing sounded like the next step, except she was worried he would be a distraction. Maybe not him but the kisses. He wanted to help, not be another obstacle to her racing. That was why earlier he'd shot from the hip, rather his lips, spouting nonsense about made-up A team celebration traditions to make her feel better. She'd known what he was doing, too. That had to be the reason she'd said no when he'd invited Brynn to hang out tonight.

A smart move on her part.

He wasn't here to mess with her.

But he'd enjoyed the way she'd pressed against him in her racing suit. Just thinking about touching her earlier sent his temperature up five degrees. Okay, ten. Welcome on a cold night, but she was correct.

More kisses would get in the way.

Not only hers. His, too.

He needed to forget about what had happened earlier. He'd been trying since saying goodbye. Except he was having trouble because Brynn was different.

And her kiss...

He'd considered the mountains his home, but with his lips against Brynn's, he'd found a new one, a place he never wanted to leave.

His stomach knotted.

What was wrong with him?

Ry knew better.

Going cold turkey with women might be his problem. Brynn was the first he'd let get close since then. But that didn't mean he wanted...

Okay, he wanted her.

But he didn't get serious, keeping things casual had been the way to go. Brynn, however, didn't seem to be the casual, let's-hang-out-and-hook-up type. Which left them nowhere to go.

"You aren't listening." Sam rocked back on his heels.

"Busty blonde in Vegas."

"Lucky guess."

Brynn and Lila laughed at something that skier said.

Ry gritted his teeth. He wanted to tell the bum to

get lost.

Wait a minute. Ry did a double take. That was the kid who came in third yesterday. A hot-shot local who'd earned an invite to one of the spring camps.

The guy was hanging on Brynn's every word. Weird, since Lila was closer to his age. The kid should put a move on her and leave Brynn alone. Except he inched closer to Brynn.

Ry didn't like it. "Why is that teenager still hanging around Brynn and Lila?"

"Because they are enjoying his company." Sam smirked. "I know you gave up alcohol, but a soda might calm you down."

"I'm calm."

Sam rolled his eyes. "Every time you see Brynn talking to that kid, your nostrils flare like a bull ready to stampede."

"Yeah, right."

A get-real expression flashed on Sam's face. "Don't tell me nothing's going on between you two."

"I'm not here to get a date."

"Given the territorial pissing match I sense coming in the next two minutes, I'd say you're past the dating phase."

As if hit, Ry flinched. He had no idea what Sam was talking about. "I've only been here three days."

"Lust knows no timeframe." Sam smirked. "And you *know* her."

At the innuendo in Sam's voice, Ry cringed. His

fault for what he'd said five years ago, but still… He needed to stop this. Now. "I told you yesterday. Nothing happened."

"You did, but she keeps glancing your way and you're ready to stake a claim, so something is definitely going on with you two now."

Ry's gaze flew to Brynn, who had turned her back to him. "Very funny."

Sam laughed. "You just proved my point. Stop fighting and surrender now. Worse ways to go. And the two of you look like a couple."

"Couple," like "commitment," was a word Ry wanted to avoid. He'd been ready for that once, but the future he'd imagined had been nothing but a pipe dream. Pippa, the woman he thought he'd spend the rest of his life with, had wanted him to give up skiing before Sochi and take his rightful place at Guyer Gear. All she'd cared about was the money to be made at his family's company, not his dreams of representing his country at the Winter Games. Ry had been devastated, but he'd thrown himself into skiing even though he could have easily lost his focus if not for friends like Henry Davenport keeping him on track.

That was why his path—his life for the next three years—was set. Nothing would change that. Why take the chance of another failed relationship knocking him off track when so much was at stake?

Bottom line, he couldn't. Even if he found Brynn

attractive with oh-so-kissable lips.

No partying. No alcohol. No women.

Making those vows had been working for him, allowing him to focus on his physical and mental well-being. Nothing had set him back so far. There was no reason to change or amend his plan. Which was why as soon as Ry finished helping Brynn, he would focus on his recovery.

"But given the age of that kid"—Sam motioned to the trio—"he has only one thing on his mind."

Ry laughed. "You might be older, but you have the same thing on *your* mind. Lila is around his age."

Sam frowned. "Lila's a kid herself. Too young to have her heart broken by some punk."

A weight pressed on Ry's chest. Brynn had been the same age as Lila when she'd been in his hotel room. His throat thickening, he rubbed his chin. "Let's make sure the guy stays in line with the ladies."

"I'm in," Sam said.

Ry headed over, forcing his way between Brynn and the teenager. "Quite the party."

She eyed him warily. "I thought you were staying at your condo tonight."

"I dragged him out." Sam was the perfect wingman and knew exactly what to say. Way better than Dwyer, who wanted to be the center of attention. Sam focused on Lila. "How ya doing, kiddo?"

The condensation from Lila's long exhale hung

on the cold air. "Just peachy."

"Ry. Sam," Brynn said. "Have either of you met Kaden?"

Kaden rocked back in his expensive snow boots. "Hey."

The kid was younger than Ry had realized, eighteen at the most. Too young for Brynn. He also recognized Kaden's admiration after years of dealing with fans. "Good job in the super combined."

"Thanks." As Kaden's face reddened, he extended a gloved hand. "Didn't know you'd be here. It's an honor, dude."

Ry supposed *dude* was better than being called *sir.* "Good luck with the rest of your events."

"Hey, you never wish *me* luck," Sam accused.

"I did yesterday."

Sam hesitated as if trying to remember. "That was the first time, and I've known you forever."

Was that true? Ry had no idea. He'd enjoyed wishing Brynn luck, but a kiss on the cheek would never be enough now that he'd tasted her lips. Except he wasn't supposed to be thinking about kisses.

He focused on Sam. "Never thought you needed any luck, but I knew you were gunning for Chas so I figured it couldn't hurt."

Smiling, Sam stood taller.

Brynn sighed. Lila beamed.

A text notification buzzed.

Kaden pulled out his phone. His face fell.

"Oh, man. I lost track of time. I gotta go or my dad will kill me for being late." Kaden's crush-filled gaze lingered on Brynn. "See ya tomorrow."

Kaden hurried away, weaving through the crowd of people.

"Nice guy?" Sam asked.

Lila shrugged. "Yeah, but a little young."

Ry moved closer to Brynn. "Enjoying yourself?"

"It's been a good break." Her voice sounded normal, but she didn't meet his gaze. "I'm ready to head to my room and relax."

"I'll go with you," he said.

Her eyebrows lowered. "That's unnecessary."

"No, but escorting you to your hotel is the gentlemanly thing to do."

"I have Lila." Brynn looked around before sighing. "Well, I had her."

Ry saw Sam and Lila strolling into a coffee shop. "They must be thirsty."

"I'm sure that was Lila's idea."

"Or Sam's." Ry shoved his hands into his jacket pockets. "Sam thinks something's going on between us."

Brynn's mouth tightened. "Did you set him straight?"

"Tried, but I'm not sure he believes me."

Brynn shook her head. "Lila's the same, but she can be devious when she wants something. I wouldn't put it past her to use what they think is happening between us to spend time with Sam."

"He's a good guy." Ry wanted to reassure Brynn because she sounded concerned. "Lila will be fine."

"She's not the one I'm worried about."

He laughed. "Sam can take care of himself. He's been around the block a time or two."

"Like you?"

"Of course." Ry fell in step with Brynn. "Not sure what kind of protection Sam has, but I've got a fortress built around this heart of mine. Keeps it safe and sound."

"Unbreachable?"

"Impenetrable." He kept his tone light as if joking, even if he was serious.

"Whatever works for you." Except she didn't sound impressed. Not surprising because most women he knew preferred to follow their hearts, not protect them. But why change what worked for him?

As they walked, the crowds lightened. She didn't talk, and he didn't feel the need to start a conversation. The silence was comfortable, not awkward. That was strange because he usually didn't like the quiet when he was with others.

"Why'd you step between Kaden and me?" she asked finally.

"Kaden has a crush on you."

Her gaze sharpened. "What's it to you?"

Ry couldn't go all caveman, even if she brought out that instinct in him for some reason. "Just watching out for you."

"I can do that myself."

She shouldn't have to. "Friends help each other out."

"Is that what we are? Friends?"

That was all they could be. "Friends and teammates. The kid seemed to be bugging you."

"And you walking me home isn't?" She shot him a questioning gaze. "I've got the super G tomorrow, but you're all I can think about, and I have no idea what to do."

Her bluntness surprised him. He wasn't used to that, but her openness appealed to him at a gut level. "I'm not here to get in your way. What do you need from me?"

"I don't suppose kissing you again would do much good."

His pulse ratcheted, well beyond his targeted heart rate. A good thing no one was monitoring him. He knew what his answer should be, but suddenly playing it safe didn't appeal to him.

Besides, it was only a kiss. "Who knows? But if you're game, so am I."

Was Brynn game for another kiss? *Yes. Yes. Yes.*

But that didn't mean she *should* kiss Ry. She had to keep her head, do what was best for her racing, not what she wanted. Ry had kept her from dwelling on her parents, but that was no reason to make him a bigger distraction, one that could affect her performance tomorrow.

"On second thought." She forced herself not to meet his gaze. If she did, she might forget her resolve not to kiss him. "Let's forget I brought this up."

"Why?"

One glimpse at his lips and her mind went blank. "I…"

"You need to concentrate on your race tomorrow," he finished for her.

His brain was functioning. Unlike hers, which short-circuited whenever he was around. That didn't happen with friends or teammates. At least it hadn't until Ry. "Yes."

She picked up her pace, eager to say goodnight.

"Hey. Slow down," he called out. "The sidewalk is slick. You don't want to fall."

Brynn stopped and waited for him to catch up. People maneuvered around them, heading toward the street party.

He wasn't limping, not that she noticed, but he moved carefully.

Oh, no. She hadn't considered his injured leg, only herself. Her mouth tasted bitter—a combination of guilt and regret. "Sorry. I wasn't thinking."

"I was guilty of that earlier."

When they'd kissed.

The words were unspoken but implied.

He caught up to her. "But I'm not sorry about kissing you. Even if I should be."

Butterflies filled her stomach. Ones that seemed to be directionally challenged given the chaos in her belly. Being near him left her unsettled. Not the icky feeling when she'd left his hotel room so long ago. More on edge, a bit...flustered.

Time to pull herself together.

Being hot and bothered around Ry wouldn't cut it. She took the shoveled pathway through the snow to where she was staying.

"It doesn't matter. You've sworn off women." Brynn arrived at the front door. "No need to crank up the charm."

"Just being honest, the way you were a minute ago. You would shut me down if I tried to charm you. In fact, you have."

She stepped aside to let people exit the building. "When?"

"That morning in the hotel was the first time," he admitted. "The last was a few minutes ago when I was hoping you wanted another kiss."

Brynn wasn't sure what to think. "More honesty?"

"That's what you want, isn't it?" He sounded sincere.

I don't know. She felt so uncertain around him.

"Yes," she answered anyway. Except now she was

the one not being totally honest. "What do you want from me?"

He removed his hands from his pockets. "You never accepted my apology for how I treated you before. Any chance you could forgive me for being such a jerk to you back then?"

Their past blared like a warning buzzer, a big red flag she couldn't ignore. Or forget. Unless he was taking care of her or talking to her or kissing her or...

Ry had gone above and beyond to help her, done nothing to make her think he was the same player he'd been. Was it time to put the past behind her for good?

She looked up at him. "If I say yes, will anything change?"

"What do you mean?"

Her turn to be honest. "Will you stick around for the rest of the week or take off?"

He moved closer to her. "I'm here until you finish your last race."

Good. Brynn enjoyed having him around. "I accept your apology."

"Yes." He pumped his hand like her brothers would do.

Men...

Though this one wasn't what she'd expected. He was special in a way she'd never imagined. That told her saying goodnight would be the smart move. She could retreat to her room, listen to music, and relax.

But staring at him made her want to stay with Ry. She could invite him inside for a few minutes. That would still give her time to think about her race...

Race day.

That came first. And would two more times this coming weekend. But after...

An idea popped into her head. *Stupid?* Yes, but she was willing to risk it.

Brynn took a breath. "How about after the giant slalom on Sunday we share some cookie dough and a few kisses?"

He leaned toward her. "I wouldn't be a distraction or bugging you then?"

"No."

Ry pushed hair off her face. "Best invitation I've had in a long time."

She wiggled her toes. "By Sunday night, I won't have to worry about racing."

And maybe they'd be celebrating a podium finish.

Or a victory.

"Can't wait," he said.

Neither could she. Brynn would enjoy tasting his kisses and the cookie dough on Sunday night. Though the one that didn't need to be refrigerated would be her favorite.

"Goodnight." Saying that was for the best. As was walking through the door alone.

His gaze lingered on hers. "Sleep well so you're rested and ready to race."

Her heart beat quicker. "I will."

Go inside.

She should, except she wasn't in a hurry to leave him.

"I'll see you in the morning," he said finally.

With that, he pushed open the door for her.

Brynn forced her feet to cross the threshold.

He smiled. "Sweet dreams."

She had a feeling her dreams would be the sweetest. Of her standing on the podium with Ry waiting to give her a victory kiss.

Chapter Nine

The next morning, patches of blue appeared in the sky, but the temperature was teeth-chattering cold. Ry stood at the bottom of the super G course with Taylor, who signed autographs and posed for pictures with fans. Only a few people recognized him, but he didn't mind. He hadn't competed in over two years. He also hadn't shaved this morning. Laziness, not because of an interview he'd read where Brynn called men with facial scruff sexy.

The announcer's voice blared over speakers, above the cowbells, horns, and cheers. The festive atmosphere was one of Ry's favorite things about ski races. That longing to be part of the competition remained, but he'd be back soon enough. "Chas showed the boys how it's done earlier. Now it's the women's turn."

Taylor's face brightened. "Regina and Ella are giving the next generation of skiers a lesson in the super G. Can't wait to see how the rest of the women do."

Especially Brynn. The super G was one of her best events, a speed race, more turns than in a downhill, but faster than a giant slalom.

She'd forgiven him, which had led to a solid night's sleep. His first since he'd arrived in Sun Valley. Now to get her a win.

"Today should be a good day for everyone," he said.

The four US alpine squads weren't the only racers attending. Skiers from all over the country were competing, including prospects who dreamed of one thing—a spot on the national team.

"Might see a few of these faces as teammates next season," he said.

Nodding, Taylor stared at the scoreboard. "I love watching the younger racers. Makes me remember when we were their age, so eager and hopeful."

Ry had been off skis long enough he felt like a newbie. So hungry to make something of himself he could taste it. "I feel the same way at the start of every season, but by the end, I'm…"

"Exhausted." They spoke at the same time and then laughed.

Traveling and living out of a suitcase for months wore a person out, even if you loved racing. Sacrifices had to be made, injuries endured.

"Still the best times ever." He'd missed being out there these past two seasons. "I wouldn't change anything."

"St. Moritz?" Taylor asked.

"Crashing out likely saved my life. I know my liver is grateful," he joked, not wanting the conversation to become too serious on what should be a fun race day.

"I'm sure your future wife will be happy with the changes you've made."

"Whoa." He held up his hands as if to ward off her words. "Let's not go crazy."

"Why not?" She sounded amused. "You and Brynn are cute together."

Cute was one thing, but he didn't have room in his life for a relationship. If he did, dating someone like Brynn might be nice. He shook the thought away.

Ry didn't have time. Once the competition was over, he was out of here.

"Are you and Chas working for Cupid now?" Ry joked, more for his benefit than Taylor's.

Her gaze softened. She squeezed his arm. "You've been through so much. I'm not just talking about your injuries and what happened after that, but I remember how badly Pippa hurt you."

His chest squeezed. Only Henry knew Ry had purchased an engagement ring and was planning to propose before she broke up with him. He and Pippa had been spoiled and used to getting what they wanted, which was why her breaking up had wrecked him. "That was a long time ago. I got over her."

"Did you? Because you haven't been in a serious relationship since Pippa." Taylor's gaze darkened. "I also haven't noticed you with anyone other than Brynn when you usually have a model or snow bunny on your arm. That's not like you."

Taylor had seen him with many women over the years. Some stuck around longer than others, but none of the relationships meant anything. At least not for him.

"It is now," he answered honestly.

She raised a brow as if she didn't believe him.

"Whatever you might think, I've been over Pippa for years." She may have destroyed his dreams of getting married and having a family, but she hadn't touched his goal of competing in Sochi. Her dumping him allowed Ry to be pinpoint-focused on skiing. Which was why he knew remaining single was the best path to take until after Beijing. "I'm choosing not to date at the moment because of my recovery."

He sounded defensive. Okay, he was. But if anyone understood where he was coming from,

Taylor would.

She touched his arm with her gloved hand. "Understandable because you want to ski, but Chas and I want you to be happy."

Her concern touched something inside Ry, but his friends had worried enough about him.

Ry raised his chin. "I'm happy."

Her brow arched.

"I *am*." He enjoyed being in Sun Valley and having fun. This break from PT and the gym was good. Seeing old friends. Making new ones. "But I'll be happier when I'm skiing again."

"It won't be long, and it'll be the best feeling ever."

He hadn't been there after Taylor's surgery, but he'd never heard her complain about not being able to race because of her knee. "Can't wait."

A relaxed smile graced her lips. "Been a wild ride for us."

"Yes, but you're living the fairy tale now." Another skier bobbled on the same part of the course where a skier had crashed out earlier. He glanced at Taylor. "You got the gold, and the guy, and left the rest of us fellows hung out to dry."

"What can I say?" she joked. "There's only one Chas."

"A good thing or none of us would win again."

She laughed. "Brynn's coming up."

This morning, Ry hadn't wanted to get in her way

or distract her so he'd skipped the team meeting. A part of him missed wishing her good luck, but the last thing she needed was anything on her mind but the race.

The crowd cheered.

On the big screen, he watched her ski the upper portion of the course. "Come on, baby."

Taylor's brows shot up. "Baby?"

Ry had no idea where that term of endearment had come from. He backtracked. "Figure of speech."

Brynn flew through the curves. Fast. Not out of control, but on edge. She came out of a turn off-balance.

He ground his teeth. "Hold it together."

She spun.

Ry's muscles bunched.

Taylor clutched his arm. "Oh, no."

Brynn went over a roll, caught air. A pole flew over her head. She landed and fell on her left side. Her skis remained attached to her boots. She slid toward the fence.

Time seemed to slow. Watching, unable to help, made him feel useless. His stomach sank to his feet. His heart, too.

Holding his breath, Ry willed her to stop. A futile wish. He'd been in a similar situation, except he'd been unconscious, unable to do anything. Someone showed him the video once. He couldn't watch the entire clip because he'd thrown up.

The slope could be unforgiving to skiers, conscious or not. Control didn't exist. Brynn was at the mountain's mercy.

She hit a bump and bounced into the air. Somehow she landed on her skis.

He stared in disbelief. "How in the world did she manage to stand?"

"She saved her ACL and her head. She'll be bruised. But she must have a guardian angel watching out for her."

"Or a lucky charm."

Brynn waved her one pole and continued down the course, much slower than she'd been going before falling.

The crowd cheered.

Taylor let go of him. "Brynn's skiing down."

Of course she was. She had to be hurting, both her body and her pride, but pain wasn't stopping her. She wanted to salvage her season. He couldn't be prouder. Even if missing gates would disqualify her.

As Brynn reached the bottom of the course, the crowd cheered louder. The clanging cowbells hurt Ry's ears.

She continued toward her waiting teammates. Regina and Ella, currently in first and second place, ran out to meet Brynn. She said something to them. The women nodded. Ella took the lone pole, and the two skiers helped Brynn off the course.

"She's a tough one," Taylor said.

"Yes, but riding adrenaline." That could mask injuries. He pulled out his lanyard. "I need to—"

"Go." Taylor motioned him forward.

Ry didn't remember his crash or the aftermath, but the immediate attention he'd received on the mountain had saved his life. Brynn would receive top care. She didn't need him, but an urge drove him toward her. Once he heard she was okay, the sick feeling in his stomach would go away and breathing wouldn't be such an effort.

He pushed his way through the crowd, saying "excuse me" or "I'm sorry." He didn't want to be rude, but he had to get to Brynn.

At the gate, he flashed his lanyard and was allowed through.

People huddled in a circle. Ry recognized the team staff. Local medical personnel were present, too. He wanted to see Brynn, but he stood back so she could get the care she needed.

"Stop fussing." She sounded more annoyed than in pain, and relief flowed through him. "I'm a little sore. That's all."

"You will let them examine you." Barking orders as usual, Coach Frederick's voice rose over the others. "Or you can forget your next race."

Tolliver must be up top at the starting gate, so Frederick was in charge down here.

Coach could be a pain in the butt, but he took care of his team and was doing that for Brynn. Skiing through pain was more the norm than feeling one hundred percent, especially by the season's end. Every skier had bruises and scars, aches and pains. That was part of skiing. A sport Ry loved, but it was brutal on the body.

And in Brynn's case, the mind. She needed to make the most of each remaining race, hurting or not. She knew that, and so did the coaches.

EMTs took Brynn to an ambulance. The team doctor followed.

"Guyer!" Frederick yelled.

"I'm going." Ry didn't need to be asked. He hated hospitals after all the time he'd been forced to spend in them, but the only place he wanted to be was with Brynn.

Wherever that might be.

Brynn had no idea what hospital they'd taken her to, but she didn't care. All she wanted was to get to the ski resort ASAP. Every second she lay in the stupid bed wearing an ugly, thin gown was a second too long. She needed to show the coaches she was good to go for tomorrow's slalom and the parallel slalom on Saturday.

Instead, she counted ceiling tiles. She'd done the same thing while waiting for X-rays. Her entire left side throbbed, the sharp pain from before dulled by medication, but nothing had taken away the ache from her hip, her legs, and her left arm.

She'd kept telling the doctors—there had been more than one based on the people in scrubs and white jackets—that nothing was broken. Ice and ibuprofen, elevation, too, and she'd be good as new, able to race tomorrow.

She'd repeated that until her voice had gone hoarse, but no one would listen to her.

Brynn hadn't hit *that* hard. Yes, the fall had hurt. Finishing the course had taken every ounce of determination she could muster. By the time she'd reached the bottom, the pain had made her woozy.

But no way had she fractured a bone.

Her knees felt okay, sore but she hadn't strained an ACL or torn a meniscus. Though she couldn't deny something was going on with her hip, more than what hurt on Monday.

Worried, she bit her lip.

But she would be fine. She had no choice if she wanted to remain on the team.

Toying with the edge of the blanket, Brynn tried to figure a creative way to tie it toga-style so she could leave the hospital without exposing her backside to everyone. She didn't want a picture of her to go viral on social media. She had nothing else to wear.

Her race suit was missing, along with the thermals she wore underneath. Her boots, socks, gloves, and pads, too. She didn't have her phone. Only her stud earrings remained.

Ry peeked his head around the curtain. "Up for some company?"

Brynn's heart squealed before banging against her rib cage. Or maybe it was the other way around, but she'd never been so happy to see someone in her life. The scruff on his face made him appear more attractive than usual. "I can't believe you're here."

Ry strode to the bed, his jacket tucked under his arm. "They wouldn't let me in, so I was stuck in the waiting room. At least there was coffee and a TV tuned to a sports channel."

He didn't sound upset, but she felt bad. "I'm sorry you missed seeing the other racers."

"I wanted to be here." He adjusted her blanket as if that was the most natural thing in the world for him to do. "What happened up there wasn't your fault."

She wished she could believe him. "I'm the one who fell."

"You weren't the only one."

"Anyone else end up in the ER?" she asked.

"No."

"Good." Brynn didn't want anyone else to have been injured. "That explains why I've had such an obscene number of tests. Must be a slow day here."

She hadn't been joking. The monitors had multiplied like fertile bunnies, one appearing after the next. Silver trays on wheels contained scary sterilized tools she didn't want touching her body. Tanks stood erect like guards at attention. She hoped no one ever needed to use one.

Brynn forced a smile. "Every single nurse has been in the room at least twice."

He pushed away the hair hanging over her eyes. "Sounds like you're in good hands."

She leaned her face against his palm. So warm and strong. Just what she needed. "I am now."

For the first time this afternoon, she could let down her guard. Nothing she said or did would be held against her. Tears welled, and she blinked them away.

"Thanks for coming." She tried sounding strong when all she wanted was a hug. "Please find me something to wear so I can leave."

Lines creased his forehead. "Not so fast. Hospitals suck. I hate them myself. But we need to know you're okay."

She hadn't followed his injury that closely, but he'd had multiple surgeries and extended hospital stays. He must have bad memories of places like this, yet he'd come anyway. For her.

Brynn's heart melted. "Ignore the gown and look at me. I'm good."

"You're beautiful, but how do you feel?"

Hearing him call her beautiful made her toes wiggle, but she doubted he would let her ignore his question. She would tell him the truth. "Sore."

"And?"

"Banged up."

"Being honest?"

In an instant she was on the mountain, catching air, feeling weightless, and then off she went. Out of control, unable to slow down, the fence looming in front of her.

"Brynn?"

"Nothing else." She blinked as if that would wipe the memory of the fall from her mind. "I'm remembering how my pulse skyrocketed when I thought I was going into the fence."

Ry laced his fingers with hers. "I've been so worried about you."

"I'll be fine." But hearing his concern touched something deep inside her. She'd only had her brothers to care about her. Knowing someone else might made her think everything would be okay.

With his free hand, he combed his fingers through her hair. "I wish I could make it better."

"You have by being here." Maybe he was feeling the same confusing thoughts about her as Brynn was about him. She studied him—from his careless, messy hat hair, killer baby blues, and lips she wanted to kiss. "You really have changed."

"I have." He squeezed her hand. "The hungover guy you once knew is no more."

"I like this guy much better."

"Same here."

Voices sounded. The curtain parted. Dr.

Gretchen Pearl, the ER doctor, entered first. Dr. Daniel Wu, one of the team physicians, followed. Their faces appeared grim.

No. No. No.

The fingers on Brynn's free hand curled into a fist. She needed to ski tomorrow.

Ry remained at her side, holding her other hand.

She appreciated his support though she hoped she didn't need it.

Dr. Wu, one of the physicians who rotated in and out of the team during the year, was new, but knowledgeable. "The X-rays are normal, Brynn. No fractures."

Thank goodness. She released the breath she hadn't realized she was holding. "Knew it."

A smile cracked Dr. Pearl's face. "I lost track of how many times you said that."

"Your bones may be fine, but you have significant bruising and a contusion. This is the second fall on your hip this week," Dr. Wu continued. "You'll stay overnight for observation. An MRI has been scheduled."

"No." The word shot from her mouth like a cannonball.

"Yes," Ry said, not missing a beat.

She glared at him. "I thought you were on my side."

"I am." He didn't let go of her hand. Instead, he tightened his grip.

"You must think this is excessive," Dr. Wu said.

Brynn nodded. "Total overkill."

"I understand, but this is the best course of action for you and your racing," he continued. "I've consulted with the team medical director, and he agrees."

That wasn't what she wanted to hear, but if it took staying here tonight so she could race, she would. "Okay."

That earned her a smile from Ry.

"The swelling should be better in a couple of days," Dr. Pearl said.

Brynn bolted upright. Grimaced in pain. "The slalom is tomorrow."

"Not possible." Dr. Wu pulled back the blanket covering her legs.

Ry flinched.

She didn't blame him. A mix of purple and black splotches colored her skin. She couldn't wear ski boots with swollen calves. "What about the parallel slalom on Saturday?"

Dr. Wu studied her bruises. "Doubtful."

Brynn's head throbbed. She'd never imagined this happening.

"The giant slalom on Sunday is a possibility," Ry said. "Right, doc?"

Of course, Ry would understand her anguish. He'd been there himself.

"You may not want to compete," Dr. Pearl said.

"But if I did?" Brynn didn't want to let go of the last shot she had at proving herself to the coaching staff. Without that...

"It's possible." Dr. Wu covered her feet with the blanket. "Let's see how you feel and if the swelling has gone down."

That was better than a no. "I'll have to console myself for missing the opening ceremony, parade, and concert tonight."

"I'll ask Amelia to take pictures for you," Dr. Wu said.

"Thanks." Brynn half laughed. "Not that I'll be missed. The spectators only want to see the A team."

"Welcome to my world," Ry joked.

"They're setting up your room," Dr. Wu said. "Dr. Pearl will see that you're settled. I'll have someone pack a few of your things and return shortly. Until then, perhaps Ry can keep you company."

He sat on the edge of her bed. "Not going anywhere, doc."

Good, because Ry made her forget all the bad stuff going on. He'd described himself as fun. Brynn might add the adjective dangerous, but he was what she needed. "Thanks."

Too bad he'd sworn off women, because a part of her would be up for more than just—she focused on their linked hands—this. A *lot* more.

Never. Going. To. Happen.

Brynn understood his priority to get on skis and

be competing with the team next season. She wouldn't want to distract him from his goals. But she would make the most of the time with him now. She had a sinking feeling when the championships ended on Sunday afternoon, all she would have left were memories of the team and of Ry.

Chapter Ten

After having an MRI, Brynn was moved to a room on the second floor. She lay in bed, hurting, but Ry's bad jokes made her laugh. Having him here kept her from getting lost in her thoughts—bad ones about what the future might hold. Though with each passing minute, the worst-case scenario seemed to be the most likely one.

Stop.

No sense borrowing worry. She'd been doing that enough.

Brynn needed to get through this overnight stay

and MRI first, and then she could deal with the fallout of the injury and her horrible season.

One step at a time.

She didn't need Ry to tell her that. He was rubbing off on her. That was good, even if she never would have believed she'd feel that way after speaking to him in the cafeteria on Monday. Had that only been three days ago?

He surveyed the room. "Not the Ritz, but it'll do for one night."

"Especially if I'm allowed to race in the giant slalom." A cheery get-well Mylar balloon was attached to the bed tray. She hunted for a note to see who'd sent it but there wasn't one. "From you?"

He shook his head. "I'm more of a candy and flowers kind of guy."

She swallowed, ignoring the flash of disappointment. What was wrong with her? Ry was here. He'd been here for hours. That was what mattered. Not gifts. Maybe the pain medication was making her loopy.

"Lucky ladies," she teased.

"My mom thinks so."

And then it hit Brynn.

Oh, no. She covered her mouth with her hand. "I need to call my mom. If she hears about this over the internet, she'll freak out, but I don't have my phone."

"Use mine." He handed her his cell phone. "I'm going to grab a hot chocolate from the cafeteria."

"Oh, that sounds good." Even with the warm blanket covering her, she was cold.

"I'll buy two." He kissed her cheek before heading out of the room.

Brynn's face tingled. She touched the spot where he'd kissed her. Her season might be in shambles and her family life a mess, but Ry kept her from losing hope.

The hungover guy you once knew is no more.

Yes, but this Ry was hotter than the younger bad boy version. A sexy image popped into her head. Not the best thought to have on her mind when she was calling her mom. She punched in the numbers.

On the second ring, the line picked up. "Hello?"

"Hi, Mom."

"Brynn! I didn't recognize the number. Thank goodness, you called. Are you okay?" Her mom spoke fast, sounding breathless.

"I'm okay." Brynn thought she heard a sigh. "I crashed out but skied down on my own. I'm sore. Have a few bruises. They're keeping me at the hospital for observation."

"What about the slalom tomorrow?"

She swallowed. "Not happening. The parallel slalom, either."

"Oh, honey."

"The giant slalom on Sunday is a possibility." Brynn kept her tone steady.

"I'm so sorry, sweetie." Her mother's voice faded.

She sounded like she was crying.

"It's okay." Brynn didn't want her mom to worry. "We've got a new doc on the team. He's being overcautious. Ordering more imaging to be on the safe side. He'll be hovering all night long."

Her mom hiccupped. "I wish I were there with you."

"Me, too." Brynn had wanted her mom so many times over the past months she'd lost count. She had no idea when she'd see her mother again. Not anytime soon if Sully had his way. Maybe not…ever. The thought stabbed Brynn's heart.

Her mom sniffled. "I've been worried sick since I heard you'd been injured."

"How did you hear?" Brynn asked.

Silence.

"Mom?"

"Your coach called me."

Brynn's insides twisted, worse than her body had during her fall. "Tolliver?"

"Mike." Her mother's breath hitched. "He knows."

The air rushed from Brynn's lungs. Her throat clogged with emotion.

He knows.

The words echoed through her head, matching the beat of her heart. All her efforts to keep her mother's secret had torn Brynn up inside and wrecked her season. How had this happened?

"I don't understand." Her voice was an octave higher. "I never said anything. You asked me not to tell him, and I didn't. I didn't tell anyone. I promise. I don't know how he would have found out."

Or when? When had he learned the truth?

He'd been acting normal. Treating her like the others on the team. Though...

After the super combined he'd been less nagging and more supportive, but she'd assumed that was because she'd finished both races. She'd even wondered if that had been a good sign she still had a shot to remain on the team.

Or had he known then?

A chill shot along her spine. She shivered.

"He told me you hadn't mentioned this to him," her mother said. "That he'd figured it out himself."

The chills racking Brynn's body had nothing to do with the ice on her leg. She pulled up the blanket to her neck. "How?"

"He didn't say, but it doesn't matter." Her mom exhaled. "He's furious at me. I tried to explain I never wanted anyone to find out for the sake of my marriage. Not even you."

"Does"—Brynn almost said *Dad*—"Sully know you kept me a secret from Mike?"

"Let's not talk about this now. You're in the hospital." Her mother's voice sharpened. "You need to concentrate on getting better so you can race."

"I've tried concentrating, focusing, you name it.

Hasn't worked. My season's ruined." Brynn's voice cracked. She didn't want to make her mom feel worse, but she couldn't keep holding everything in. "One more race won't make a difference. I'm going to lose my spot."

A vise gripped Brynn's heart. Saying that aloud made the reality of her situation clearer. This week's races wouldn't change three months of poor results.

Nothing would.

She'd been living in denial because…

She didn't deserve to be on the team, not after letting personal issues interfere with her performance. Forget about getting a spot with a coach's discretion. Her name shouldn't be on next season's nomination list. She hadn't earned a spot. Didn't deserve one. She knew with the same certainty she'd known she hadn't broken any bones today.

Life as a member of the team would end when next season's nominations came out. The most she could hope for was an invite to one of the camps to compete for a spot or be asked to train with the team as an independent, covering her own expenses. Not that she had the money to do that.

The familiar elephant, who'd been overstaying his welcome since December, plopped on her chest once more. She wanted him to get off and go away. Forever.

Brynn clutched the phone, ignoring the aches in her hip and muscles and the pain in her heart. She'd waited long enough. Too long. No more.

"Please, Mom." Brynn tried to settle her shaky hand. "I love you and know this has been rough on you, but it's been tough for me, too. You told me what you thought I needed to know, but it's not enough. I have a feeling Coach will want to talk, and I'm guessing at this point, he knows more than I do. Please don't leave me in the dark any longer."

Silence.

Unsure whether her mom would hang up or speak, Brynn clutched the cell phone.

"I told you how your dad...Sully...had been sleeping with women while on the road. I had suspicions, but no proof until a woman showed up at the house. She was so young and trusting, thought he was divorced, not married with a wife and five kids. Needless to say, I found out she wasn't the only one. We separated, and I contacted a divorce attorney."

"That must have been difficult for you."

"It was. Our marriage was far from perfect, but I never imagined myself divorced." Her mom paused. "I was so torn up, I was going to skip my friend's wedding, but your grandmother convinced me to go and see my old ski friends. So I did, never thinking Mike might be there, too."

"But he was."

"It was the first time I'd seen him in fourteen years. Not since he'd broken up with me."

"Was it uncomfortable?"

"At first yes, but then not so much." Her mom paused. "Mike was always easy to be around."

Brynn had to laugh. "That's so not the coach I know."

"People change. He had. I noticed that right away. He seemed a little off. Sad, even." Her mother sighed. "At the reception, we ended up pouring out our souls to each other over a bottle of wine. He about becoming a full-time coach. Me about my crumbling marriage to a hockey coach and my five sons. But once all that was out of the way, it was as if we'd turned back the clocks to when we'd been younger and so in love. One thing led to another and…"

"Me."

"You," her mother said at the same time. "I've never regretted that night with Mike. Or you. Forget what Sully said to you. He was wrong."

Brynn needed to hear that. "Thanks."

"When it was time for me to go home, Mike gave me his number. Told me he'd lost me once and didn't want that to happen again. Said he'd visit as soon as the divorce was final. I thought we might get a second chance together, but then Sully surprised me. When I arrived at your grandmother's house, he was there waiting, begging me not to divorce him."

There was something Brynn needed to know. "Why did you go back to him if Mike wanted to be with you?"

"Sully and I were still married, and we had five children together."

"Did you know you were pregnant with me?"

"No," her mother admitted. "Your brothers needed a father, and I was terrified of the financial repercussions of a divorce because I hadn't worked in years. That's why I called Mike and told him not to contact me again. I had no idea I was carrying his baby, you, at the time."

Brynn didn't know whether she should be happy or sad about that. She'd assumed her mom had known about the pregnancy when she spoke with Coach. "What happened after you found out about me?"

"I told Sully what had happened at the wedding, but I didn't mention Mike's name. Sully didn't ask."

"Were you afraid he'd divorce you?"

Her mom half laughed. "I had no idea what he would do."

"But you never told Coach. He—"

"Left me once because he wanted no distractions to his skiing."

That was similar to what Ry had told Brynn. A hollowness seemed to grow inside her. "Mike wasn't skiing anymore."

"Coaching takes even more time. And asking a man, a bachelor who'd probably never babysat, to welcome me and five kids into his life, and then one on the way when I found out about you, would have been too much."

Brynn grimaced. "So you chose Sully."

The safer known option.

"Yes, but working through our issues wasn't easy. We went into counseling to deal with his affairs and what happened with me and Mike. Sully admitted his wrongdoings and didn't blame me for mine. He forgave me. And I did the same with him. We each had our own requirements for staying together, and we've stuck to those all these years."

In December, her mom had told Brynn what those conditions entailed: no more cheating, Sully raising Brynn as his own child, and no contact for her mom or Brynn with the birth father. Only that last one had happened unknowingly when she'd made the national team. "You couldn't stop me from getting to know Mike Frederick."

"That was out of our control, but it won't matter. Sully doesn't know Mike's identity—"

"If he finds out…"

Her mother inhaled sharply. "That's something I'll deal with. Not you."

Brynn had a feeling her entire family would be dealing with the repercussions. She didn't know if the truth coming out now was better than if it had twenty-five years ago. "Did you ever think Coach had a right to know about me?"

"I—" Her mother's voice cracked. "I'd cut off contact with him. Threw away his number. I did what

I thought best."

"Best for the boys?"

"And you."

Brynn wished she believed that. "Sully never treated me as his own."

"What was I going to do?" Her mother sounded angry. "Call Mike and tell him he had a daughter I'd never told him about?"

"That might have been better than me growing up feeling as if I didn't belong and would never measure up because I was a girl." The words, buried inside for so long, spewed out, full of hurt and disappointment. "I tried, but nothing was ever good enough for Sully."

"Your father tried."

"Sully didn't, and you let him get away with it."

"I had to keep the family together."

"I'm part of that family," Brynn countered. "Or was until Sully kicked me out."

Silence filled her ear.

That didn't stop Brynn. "For twenty-five years, you've been worried about the effect of that night with Coach on your sons and yourself. You don't even care what keeping this secret has done to me. That I'm going to lose my spot on the team and be homeless."

"I care."

That was debatable. Brynn was hurting and too tired to fight. She'd said what she'd been holding back.

Her mother blew her nose. "If there was a way I could be there now…"

But.

Her mom always had a "but."

But it would rip the family apart.

But I wouldn't be able to see my grandkids.

But I don't want my husband to divorce me.

"But it would cost too much to fly there," her mother said finally. "Sully would never pay for an airline ticket."

Jax would. If Brynn knew that, then so did their mother.

But…

Coming west would mess up things with Sully, the five boys, and the grandchildren. Her mother would never risk it.

Brynn's breath hitched. She forced air into her lungs, but that didn't keep tears from stinging her eyes.

She was the expendable one. Always had been.

That was why she'd grown up feeling as if everyone else in her family was more important to her parents, not just Sully. But to have that fact proven now hurt more than her left side and all the angst she'd suffered since December combined.

Her hand trembled so much she nearly dropped Ry's cell phone. "I have to go, Mom."

"Call if you need anything."

I need you. Brynn had needed her mom since December, but that hadn't mattered then. It wouldn't now. "Bye."

She disconnected from the line. "Sully doesn't want me. My mom, either. I wonder if Coach will."

Brynn wiped her eyes. Probably best not to get her hopes up. She'd been disappointed enough and wasn't sure if she could handle much more.

Chapter Eleven

Ry returned to Brynn's room with two hot chocolates in a drink carrier and a small vase filled with mixed blossoms. The bright colors and sweet fragrance reminded him of Brynn. He hoped she liked them.

Cracking open the door, he didn't hear her voice, so he peeked inside.

Brynn wasn't on the phone. She lay in bed with the blanket tucked under her chin. The hot chocolate would warm her up. Other than the bulge underneath from the ice and a pillow, she didn't appear injured, but she looked so vulnerable and exhausted.

Ry approached the bed. All he wanted was to make things better for her.

"For you." He set the vase on the bed tray so she could smell the flowers, before removing one of the hot cocoas. When she didn't reach for the cup, he placed it next to the vase within arm's reach of her. "I asked for whipped cream and chocolate sauce on top. You deserve a splurge, and they were out of cookie dough."

"Th-thanks." Her voice sounded hoarse.

Her face was as white as fresh snow. Her red and puffy eyes suggested she'd been crying. He wanted to kiss away her troubles so a smile lit up her face. Instead, he went to press the call button for the nurse.

She grabbed his hand. "No."

Her pained expression reminded him of the night she talked about her parents. "Is your mom worried about you?"

"With six athletic kids, she's used to hospital visits, but that's not the issue." Brynn bit her lip. "I—I talked to her about what's been going on. There was stuff I wasn't clear about or didn't know. Now I do."

The rawness in her voice hurt his heart. Whatever she'd learned had to have been rough. Unsure what to do or say, Ry held her hand.

He wanted to help, but he also didn't want to interfere. This was her family, not his. Yet seeing her so torn up demanded he do something. He hoped being a supportive friend was enough. "You don't have to tell me."

Her lower lip trembled. "I've been keeping this secret since December. I need to talk to someone besides my mom because…"

Brynn's lower lip quivered.

He kissed the top of her hand. "I'm all yours. To listen or do whatever you need."

The gratitude in her gaze clogged his throat with emotion. She made him feel like the most important guy in the world. *Her* world. Not because of Guyer Gear or his skiing, but because he was here for her. That meant more than he could imagine.

His heart thudded. "You can trust me."

"I know."

Ry's chest filled with pride and something else. He wanted to be there for Brynn in a way he hadn't felt before. Confusing, yes, but that wouldn't stop him. He rubbed her hand with his thumb.

She took a breath and then another.

He tightened his hold on her. "Take your time."

As Brynn nodded, her lips parted. "In December, I found out that my mom's husband, Sully, isn't my birth father. I'd grown up thinking he was. But everything I believed about my family was a lie. Sully cheated on my mom. More than once. They were on the verge of divorcing when she hooked up with an old boyfriend at a wedding and got pregnant with me."

O-kay. Not the family drama he'd expected to hear. But, wow. No wonder Brynn couldn't focus on her races. "That explains your being distracted."

Her jaw clenched. "After Lake Louise, Sully said hurtful things. That I'm not part of his family and no longer welcome in his house. He packed up my things and sent them to Jax."

As Brynn reached for her cocoa, her fingers trembled. He let go of her hand so she could use both to hold the cup. Carefully, she took a sip of her drink. "This is good."

A dollop of whipped cream was on her upper lip. Now wasn't the time for fun or flirting or licking it off. He used his finger instead.

She smiled at him.

His stomach fluttered. Needing to touch her, he rested his palm on her shoulder.

"Three months ago, I'd asked my mother to tell me what happened and received the condensed version. I learned my birth father's name and that my mom hadn't told him she was pregnant. She asked him not to contact her again so she could save her marriage. My mom begged me not to tell anyone for the sake of our family so I've been keeping her secret."

Ry's muscles tensed. "Your mom shouldn't have put this on you. You're innocent in all this. What's going on is between her and her husband."

Staring into the hot cocoa, Brynn dragged her

upper teeth over her lower lip. "I wish that were true, but there's more."

Okay, he needed to shut up and let her talk. "Go on."

"I just found out that my birth father knows about me," she continued. "He called my mom after I was injured today."

"He's here in Sun Valley?" Ry had no idea why she was staring so intently at him. "Brynn?"

"Did you talk to Coach Frederick about me?" There was an urgency to her question.

Coach must know her dad. Ry rubbed his chin, trying to remember when they'd spoken about her. "It was yesterday, after the team meeting. He asked how you were doing."

She placed her cup on the bed tray. "What did you tell him?"

"That you were dealing with family issues. It was weird, though."

"Weird, how?"

"I mentioned your brothers. He'd met two and thought that's all you had." Ry remembered Coach's expression. "He didn't know your dad was a coach and you had five brothers who are all into hockey, but he took off right after that so nothing else was mentioned."

Not unusual for Frederick, except Brynn's forehead was creased. She breathed faster.

Wait. That didn't mean...

No, it couldn't be. That kind of news would lead to tabloid headlines for the team.

But if it were true, that could explain why Coach hurried away. "Coach Frederick…"

"…is my father."

"Coach?" Ry let the news sink in. "That's…"

"Crazy. Insane. And lots of other things."

Ry scrubbed his hand over his face. "If people find out…"

"They might believe Coach knew all along. He could be accused of things. None of which are true because he's never played favorites with any of us, and until this year, I've always met the selection criteria to be on the team. But some won't see it that way."

Careful of her left side, Ry wrapped his arm around her. "I'm so sorry."

Her eyes gleamed. "I don't want Coach or the team hit with bad publicity. That's another reason I haven't said anything."

She was protecting her mother, her brothers, Coach Frederick, and the team. But who was watching out for Brynn? No wonder her season had fallen apart.

Ry, however, had added to her troubles. "I'm sorry I mentioned your family to Coach."

She leaned against him, grimaced, and then straightened. "You have nothing to apologize for. I don't blame you. You had no idea what was going on.

I'm the one who should have kept my mouth shut."

"I don't know how you've dealt with this secret on your own and raced."

"I haven't done a very good job." She touched the blanket covering her legs "Especially today."

"You're lucky you finished some races and only DQ'd from others, not…" Ry stared at her in the hospital bed. Heat flushed through his body. Red, hot, angry heat. His nails dug into his palms. He forced himself to breathe. "You could have killed yourself racing when you were so distracted. Not just today. Any day you were out there."

"But I didn't. I'm very much alive."

"No thanks to your mom or Sully." The realization of what might have happened to Brynn pummeled Ry. Knees weak, he sat on the edge of her bed. The thought of anything worse happening to her slayed him. His parents had said they would have traded spots with him in the hospital. He'd never understood how they'd felt until now. Or why his mom and dad became so concerned when Ry talked about racing again. "I don't know if I should be mad at you for continuing to race or kiss you for being so strong."

"If you kiss me, be gentle." She sounded lighthearted, but her expression was dark and troubled. "Everything hurts, including my face."

He brushed his lips over hers with feather-light softness. "Okay?"

She nodded once.

The phone rang, shaking the bed tray with its ring and vibration. He checked at the screen. "The area code is seven zero two."

"Vermont. My mom." Brynn grabbed his hand. "Please don't leave."

"I won't." She needed someone to watch out for her. He would.

"Hello," she said into his phone. "You told me you wouldn't be coming, Mom... Yes, that is expensive... No, I'm not alone. A friend is here... Yes, from the team. Okay. I'll call you after I'm released. Bye."

"You're more bummed now."

Brynn handed him the phone. "I don't know why my mom called again. She used the cost of the ticket as the reason she's not flying out even though Jax would pay for it. He has more money than he knows how to spend. I've been injured worse, but I would love to have her here for moral support."

Ry combed his fingers through her hair. "Totally understandable."

"Sully is the real reason she won't come. He doesn't know who my birth father is, but she promised Sully she'd never see Coach again. And she hasn't. That's why she doesn't attend my races if the men and women compete together."

"I'm sorry." Ry didn't know what else to say. He couldn't imagine being in Brynn's situation, but the need to protect her became stronger.

"Everything my mom's doing is for Sully and my brothers. It's always been that way. But that became clearer today." Brynn had a faraway expression on her face. "Once, just once, I wish I didn't feel like an afterthought. I want to come first. That must sound selfish."

Ry hated thinking how Brynn must have wondered why her mom didn't attend many races. She must have felt ignored and unloved. Forgotten. "Not at all."

Brynn sipped her cocoa. "My mom said Coach chose skiing over her once, and she wouldn't risk him making the same choice again. That's why she never told him."

About me was left unspoken.

"Your mom made a choice of her own."

"She did what was best for my brothers and her marriage. Not once did she consider what was best for me." As Brynn's voice faded, hurt slashed through Ry at the heartache in her eyes. "Growing up, I thought Sully didn't know how to deal with a daughter because he was so distant. My brothers got all the attention. Nothing I did was ever good enough. But my mother let me keep trying and failing. Even though she knew why he felt the way he did. That hurts worse than any bruise or contusion. I was so alone. Still am."

"You're not alone." Ry scooted closer. "I'm

here."

He would do whatever he could to make things better for her. She was giving everything she had, including her skiing career, for her family. But they weren't doing anything in return.

He'd felt helpless sitting in the waiting room, and again when he'd been in the examining room, but now he knew how to help her. His dad had a jet. If Ry couldn't get access to that, he had money, and like her brother, more than Ry could ever spend. "I'll get your mom here."

"No, this isn't your problem."

"You need your mom." He could do this one small thing.

"If she wanted to be here, she would be on her way. I'll be okay." Brynn's tears hit him like a left hook. She blinked, staring at the ceiling. "You're here. The team, too."

That wasn't enough. Helping Brynn felt natural, right. No matter what she'd said, he wanted to do this for her. At least try.

"Rest." Ry brushed his lips over her hair. Comforting her was the most natural thing in the world. "You need to heal. Everything else can wait until you feel better."

The tension seemed to seep out of her body. Her eyelids appeared heavy. "I'm so happy you're with me."

She sounded sleepy. The pain medicine must be

kicking in. He hoped she napped. "I'm not going anywhere."

"Good, because I enjoy having you around."

Ry felt the same way. He hadn't come to Sun Valley to find forever, but *right now* sounded great. He hoped that would be enough.

For both of them.

An hour passed. The hospital bed made for a cozy fit, but Ry didn't mind. Brynn slept soundly, her breathing more even than before, but he felt an occasional twitch or jerk.

Bad ones, if his own accident was anything to go by.

Ry rubbed her right arm with his free hand, careful not to press so he wouldn't hurt her. Brynn's skin was warm and soft. She appeared vulnerable, as fragile as a glass sculpture.

But she wasn't.

Brynn Windham was a strong, beautiful, sexy woman, who should be on the podium, not in the hospital. He was thankful she hadn't been injured worse. Today or during one of her earlier races. She'd sacrificed her season and spot on the team to keep her mother's secret.

That shouldn't have been her responsibility.

Not fair.

But life wasn't.

Brynn lay under the covers. Ry was on top of them on purpose.

He hadn't been this physically close to a woman in over two years, and the gown she wore left little to his imagination. He didn't want to be the old Ry-Guy, always thinking about what a woman could give him. He wanted to be here for Brynn, to help her, to give to her.

Yes, part of his making amends even though she'd forgiven him. But holding her, watching her sleep, had never made him feel so…so content. He didn't know how to explain the feeling, so he didn't try.

The door to the room opened. Dr. Wu had been in and out, as had two nurses.

Ry looked over to see who it was this time. "Coach?"

Mike Frederick entered the room wearing his race day gear—ski pants and an unzipped team jacket. No hat or gloves, but two cinch sacks were on his shoulder. He also carried a bag from the ski resort's gift shop.

Coach appeared wary, which wasn't like him, but in a second, his expression hardened. His face reddened. Both were familiar signs of anger from the well-respected leader of the men's alpine team. "Unless Dr. Wu ordered you to be that close to Brynn, get out of her bed and stay off."

A throbbing blood vessel appeared as if it might pop on Frederick's forehead.

Yeah, this wasn't a normal reaction from the man.

Best to do what he wanted.

Ry slid from the bed, careful not to wake Brynn, but not slow enough to piss off Coach more. "Better?"

"Not really." Coach lowered his voice. The soft volume was the antithesis of how he chastised skiers, but that didn't stop him from pinning Ry with a glare. "You're still too close to her."

Overprotective much? He wished Brynn was awake so she could witness Coach going all father-of-a-daughter on Ry. At least that was what appeared to be happening.

"You don't have to whisper. We won't disturb her." As Ry crossed to the other side of the room to appease the man who held the future of his skiing in the palm of his hand, he glanced at the bed. Brynn hadn't moved. "She's exhausted and on pain medication. I doubt she'll wake up for a while."

Coach's nostrils flared. "I asked you to help Brynn, not—"

"I've *been* helping her." A couple of kisses weren't anyone's concern. Ry kept his voice soft. "Nothing else."

Coach lifted a single brow. "You expect me to believe you?"

"Yes." Ry didn't miss a beat. "Brynn's been dealing with so much on her own. She needed someone, and I was here. Like *you* asked me to be."

Coach appeared to want to say more, but his lips

pressed together.

Interesting. Frederick was known for speaking his mind and then apologizing later if need be. He approached the side of Brynn's bed. "How is she?"

"Sore. Sad." Ry forced himself not to look at her. "Unsure what will happen."

Coach ran a hand over his messy hair. Brown strands mixed with gray ones stuck up every which way. He blew out a puff of air. "I'm not sure, either."

The reply shocked Ry. Coach was a living search engine of alpine skiing knowledge, know-how, and wisdom. He exuded strength and confidence, no matter what, and often shared personal tidbits and stories to drive home a point about something he wanted a skier to consider. As long as Ry had known Coach, which had been for over a decade, he'd never seen Mike Frederick uncertain about anything.

Until finding out about Brynn.

Ry didn't know if Coach was confused or upset or a combination. No matter what the man was feeling, Ry would protect Brynn. She'd lost one family over something completely out of her control. He wouldn't allow Coach to hurt her, too. Not on Ry's watch.

"Tonight, she told me about you and her." Ry glanced at Brynn before focusing on Coach. "She's been trying to keep who her father is a secret since December. That was when Brynn found out from Sully that he wasn't her father. Her mother told her the truth, but since then, Brynn has been trying to keep your identity to herself because that's what her mom wanted. That's the reason she lost her focus this season, but I had no idea about any of this when I talked to you yesterday."

A range of emotions—from frustration to embarrassment—crossed Coach's face. He touched Ry's shoulder gently, the same way Coach had done when Ry had been in the hospital. "It's not your fault. You gave me enough information to connect the dots. The truth would have come out, eventually. Keeping that secret was too much for Brynn to handle on her own. She's lucky she didn't kill herself skiing with all this in her head."

"I told her the same thing, but she was protecting her family and the team. She told me you didn't know."

"Hadn't a clue."

"I won't tell anyone. This messed up Brynn's season. I won't do anything to screw it up more and hurt her. I hope you won't, either."

Coach's gaze narrowed. "I might not have known about her, but now that I do, I… I don't know what to do, but I won't hurt her. You have my word."

"I believe you."

He stared at her. "She has her mother's smile. Funny how I never noticed the resemblance to Deanna."

"Look closer." Ry took a step toward the bed. "You might find something that reminds you of yourself."

"Brynn's a better skier than Deanna and me combined."

"Mrs. Windham is flying in tomorrow."

Coach nearly jumped. "Deanna told me she couldn't come."

"Change of plans, but Brynn doesn't know yet. I made the arrangements while she was sleeping." His father's plane was being used so an airplane ticket had been purchased, a hotel room reserved, and a ride from the airport booked. "Mrs. Windham arrives in the late afternoon."

Coach pinched the bridge of his nose as if he were trying to hold himself together. Guess the man was human and had blood running through his veins, not ice as the team believed.

He lowered his hand. "Brynn needs her mom."

"And her dad." Ry fought the urge to touch Brynn, but he didn't want to upset Coach, who fidgeted with the handle on the bag. "She needs a father."

Coach drew back, his mouth falling open. "She has one. Deanna's husband."

"That jerk treated her like an ugly stepchild the entire time she was growing up even though he claimed to be her father. He wasn't physically abusive from anything she said, but verbally…" Ry's blood boiled thinking about what she'd been through. "In December, he kicked her to the curb. He won't let her come home again. Packed her stuff and sent it to one of her brothers."

As Coach's brows drew together, he frowned. "Deanna's allowed that to happen?"

"Sounds like it from what Brynn said. She's strong, but she's been through so much." Too much. That made Ry think of something else he needed to say to Coach. "You need to get along with her mom."

He flinched. "Get along?"

Ry didn't understand why Coach sounded so offended. "Yeah. She said you and her mom hooked up at a wedding."

He shook his head rapidly. "You make it sound like a one-night stand between two strangers. It wasn't."

"No?"

"Not at all." He studied Brynn. "I've been in love with her mother for nearly forty years. I lost Deanna the first time because I chose skiing over her. We were young. Too young, I thought. The second time…she never gave me the choice. I was planning on us being together once her divorce was final. I wasn't sure what kind of stepfather I'd be, but I wasn't going to lose her again. But then she called and said she was going back to her husband and to not contact her again, so I didn't. I had no idea she was pregnant. If I'd known, I would have done things differently."

The regret in his voice matched the sadness in his

eyes. Coach Frederick had always been larger than life, but now he seemed exposed…all too human.

"You've had a great career, both as a skier and a coach. Now you also have a daughter. She's been abandoned enough. If you walk out on her—"

"I won't." Coach moved toward her bed. "Deanna and I will figure this out and make sure we help our daughter. Brynn won't be on her own."

Relief flowed through Ry. "Thank you."

"Thank you for caring about what happens to Brynn." Her hair spread across the white pillowcase. With a tentative hand, Coach touched a few strands before jerking away as if he touched a flame. "I wish she came with an instruction manual."

Ry bit back a laugh. "That would help, but give it time. You'll both need that."

Nodding, Coach pressed his arms against his sides as if forcing himself not to reach out to her again. "Go, eat dinner. I'll stay in case she wakes up."

"Thanks." Ry moved to the door, trying to reconcile this Coach with the one who demanded one hundred and fifty percent from his skiers. "Do you want anything from the cafeteria?"

"No, thanks." He moved a chair closer to the bed. "I'll grab something later."

Coach sat and stretched his legs out. He reminded Ry of his own father who had done the same during numerous hospital visits. Brynn's situation made Ry realize how lucky he was to have parents who cared the way his did.

Maybe Ry would call his father after he ate, tell him about Brynn, and see how things were going at home and Guyer Gear. That was the least he could do for the man who had always been there and loved him unconditionally.

Something Brynn hadn't had from Sully. Maybe she'd have Coach's support from now on.

Ry sure hoped so.

After all she'd been through, Brynn deserved that kind of love from a parent, if not two of them.

Chapter Twelve

Brynn's entire body ached. She opened her eyes to find the lights in the hospital room dimmed. She didn't know how long she'd been sleeping, but it hadn't been enough. One thing was different. Ry was no longer next to her. She missed his warmth. He might be the most attractive man she'd ever seen, but his caring heart trumped his handsome face.

You're not alone. I'm here.

Affection for him overflowed. But where was he?

"You're awake."

Brynn stiffened. Pain sliced through her bruised

muscles. Coach Frederick sat in a chair on the other side of the bed. "I didn't know anyone was here."

"Dr. Wu's been in and out. I sent Ry to eat dinner." Coach pointed to a cinch sack on the counter. "Amelia packed some things for you. Lila gave her your cell phone. Though it may have exploded with all the text messages. The team wants to see you, but I told them not until after the slalom tomorrow."

"Thanks." This was the Mike Frederick she respected, the take-charge coach who ran a tight team and took care of the skiers. Nothing distracted him. Not even knowing he had a daughter. She swallowed. "How did everyone do today?"

"Top three for Regina, Ella, and Lila."

"That's great for them." Brynn hoped she sounded excited because she was. She hated being in the hospital, but her teammates' podium finishes pleased her. "Coach Tolliver must be thrilled."

This was awkward. Beyond skiing, Brynn had no idea what to say. Mike Frederick had seen her at her best and her worst but always as a coach. Even though he knew about being her father, she wasn't sure how to bring up anything not involving skiing. "Coach…"

"Brynn," he said at the same time.

Heat rushed up her neck. She peered down at the blanket covering her.

"You go first," he said finally.

Inhaling slowly, she raised her gaze to meet his. "Did you ever...think about my mom?"

"Yes." He didn't hesitate to answer. "More than you can imagine. I...cared about her."

He sounded sincere. That was good. "Did you think there could have been a baby after...?"

"Honestly, no," he admitted. "Never crossed my mind."

Of course not, since her mom had told him not to contact her and then kept the pregnancy a secret. Brynn had known that, but she'd needed to hear from him.

"This isn't a situation I thought I'd find myself in." As he brushed his hand through his hair, an exasperated expression crossed his face. "I'm not close to being over the shock of finding out about you."

Shock. Not excitement.

Brynn's heart seemed to rip in half. Her body tensed again, sending more slivers of pain through her. Squeezing her eyes closed, she waited for disappointment to hit. Regret and anger, too. A numbness, however, set in as if each nerve ending had gone into hibernation. Self-preservation? Or perhaps the nurse had given her extra pain meds when she was asleep. Brynn should be freaking out and throwing herself a pity party because Coach didn't want her, either.

Unless she'd reached the point of acceptance.

Many people didn't have fathers. Some through no fault of their own. Others by choice. Having Sully out of her life would be better for Brynn in the long run. She could shrug off the blame she'd carried for never being enough for him and repair the damage he'd caused to her self-esteem and confidence. As for Coach...

She'd lived without her biological father her entire life. Even though she loved the idea of having a dad, the reality of that was a big unknown. Other than how she saw Sully with her brothers, she didn't know what having a father meant. It appeared she never would.

He touched her right shoulder. "I'll get the nurse."

Brynn opened her eyes. "That's not necessary."

"You're in pain."

"I'm sore, but it's not my injuries." She didn't feel comfortable saying more. After a lifetime of rejection from Sully, she wouldn't make the same mistake with Coach by forcing a relationship or trying too hard to please him.

Brynn was tougher than she realized and would get through this, albeit not without scars, but she would survive. She finally realized, except for Jax and Ace, no one else had considered her part of the family. She adjusted her blanket.

"I'm not sure what girls like, and you're not a girl anymore but..." Coach picked up something from beside his chair, stood, and handed her a stuffed

Siberian husky dog. "This is for you. I thought it was a good idea at the time."

Her breath hitched. "Thanks."

Holding the animal against her chest, a ball of warmth formed around her heart. No matter what happened, even if they never spoke about her being his daughter again, she would cherish this gift from him.

Not once had Sully bought her anything beyond food and school clothing. Her brothers had top-of-the-line skates and gear. She'd worn her brothers' hockey hand-me-downs when she'd played. Her ski equipment had been used, purchased with grocery money her mom had set aside each week. Once Brynn was old enough to babysit, she'd been told to buy her own stuff. It hadn't seemed right given how expensive playing hockey at the highest levels cost, but nothing in her childhood had been fair. Life wasn't.

A snowball-sized lump formed in her throat.

Coach shifted his weight between his feet. "I have no idea what I'm supposed to do or say, Brynn. I'm a coach. I know alpine skiing. This is… I'm not sure what this is."

The numbness remained. Her fantasies about Coach Frederick taking on the father role from the beginning had died the moment he mentioned being shocked. Not that she was surprised. Real life seldom came out as wonderful as one's daydreams. But he was still her coach for now. Focusing on being one of his skiers and nothing else would be best.

As she raised her chin, she ignored the pain on the left side of her face. "Nothing has to change…"

"Is that what you want?"

"I…" Brynn was afraid to answer. She might be strong, but a person could only take so much disappointment. She'd exceeded her quota, and the season wasn't over yet. "I don't want to be a burden."

"You're not," he answered quickly but firmly. "But I need time."

That was more than she thought he'd say. She nodded, which hurt, too.

"It's always been just me. On my own. I'm going to make mistakes." He cleared his throat. "I made Ry get out of your bed earlier."

She'd heard Frederick tell Dwyer to stay away from the younger women on the team. "That's something a coach would say."

"True, but I wasn't feeling like your coach when I said it."

An unexpected thrill shot through her. Maybe she *would* have a dad or a father figure. Not today or tomorrow, but someday. The kernel of hope was enough for now. "There's no rush to figure this out."

"No, but we will." He reached for her before pulling his arm to his side. "I promise."

A promise was more than she'd gotten from either Sully or her mom. Brynn cuddled the stuffed dog. "Thanks."

♥ ♥ ♥

After dinner, Ry returned to the room on the second floor. The scene was similar to when he'd left—Coach sitting in the chair staring at Brynn asleep in the bed. The only difference was the stuffed animal against her chest. Ry hadn't seen that before.

He'd been thinking about Brynn while he ate. Okay, she'd been on his mind all day, not only here at the hospital, but now he wanted to move closer, touch her. Because of Frederick, he kept his distance. "How is she?"

"Sore." Coach straightened. "Brynn woke up for a short time before falling asleep again."

That didn't tell Ry what he wanted to know. He shifted his weight between his feet. *Might as well ask.* "Things go okay between the two of you?"

"It'll take time."

That didn't sound good, but Ry saw no tissues on the bed tray, so he assumed tears hadn't fallen. That was good given how upset she'd been after speaking with her mom. He wanted something to finally go Brynn's way. Nothing had the past three months.

The dark circles under Coach's eyes stood out more than they had when he arrived.

"You should go. Eat. Sleep," Ry suggested. "Tomorrow is a big day."

Coach's gaze remained on Brynn. "She shouldn't be alone."

"I'm staying. That's why the guys sent clothes for me."

His expression hardened, the lines on his face deepening. Not with anger but concern. He started to speak, but Ry held up his hand.

"I'll take good care of her," Ry said. "The team needs you to be rested for the slalom. Skiers are counting on you. Brynn would want you at the course."

Coach hesitated before patting the chair arm. "You sleep here. Not on the bed."

With her was implied.

Ry nodded, but if Brynn wanted him next to her, he wouldn't say no. Coach would never find out unless a doctor or nurse mentioned it to him. Maybe Ry would stick to the chair tonight.

Coach stood. "If her condition changes or she needs me…"

"I'll call you."

His hand hovered above Brynn's arm, but he never touched her. "I should go."

As Coach headed to the door, he glanced over his shoulder at her as if he wanted one last look to make sure she was real.

Ry forced himself not to smile. "Goodnight."

He waited for the door to shut before moving closer to the bed and pushing the hair off Brynn's face. *So beautiful.* "You're going to have a dad. An overprotective one, but you'll be good for each other."

That much was obvious given Mike Frederick's concern about Brynn. One that went beyond the normal coach-athlete relationship. Ry hoped she recognized that. Or would soon.

As he smoothed her hair, his phone rang.

Brett Matthews's name flashed on the screen.

Ry raised the phone to his ear. "I doubt you're calling to tell me my portfolio is up. I'm assuming I would have heard if the market crashed."

Brett laughed. "Always the jokester, Guyer. No crash. You're making money, or I wouldn't be doing my job, but that's not why I'm calling."

The way his tone became more serious worried Ry. He pictured Brett's wife and baby girl. "Everything okay with Laurel and Noelle?"

"My family is fine," Brett replied without missing a beat. "It's Henry."

Henry Davenport, one of Ry's closest friends, had inherited billions from his late parents and never worked a day in his life. He lived in Portland near Brett, enjoyed spending money, partying with friends, and dating beautiful women. Henry also liked sticking his nose into other people's business and had recently decided his mad matchmaker skills were the reason Brett and Laurel fell in love.

"Henry was fine when I spoke with him a half hour ago," Ry said.

"He's concerned about you."

That's weird. All Ry had asked was if Brynn could stay in Henry's guest house after the season ended. She wouldn't have to pay rent and could train on Mount Hood. "Why?"

"The way you talked about Brynn reminds Henry of how you spoke about Pippa."

Ry nearly dropped his phone. He gripped the device tighter. "Henry's delusional."

"Henry's a man-child, but his heart's in the right place given what you've been through."

Ry stepped away from the bed. Henry, who was a few years older than Ry, had been the one to pick up the pieces after he'd been dumped by Pippa. Henry had also been the one to find Ry when he'd hit rock bottom while recovering from his crash and saved his life.

So maybe Henry wasn't delusional, but the guy was becoming a worrywart for nothing. "He could have called me himself."

"If he wasn't packing so he could fly to Sun Valley tonight, I'm sure he would have."

Ry swore. That was so Henry, but still... "Stop him, please."

The less Ry said, the better, or Brett might come, too. Brett knew his place and was a chill guy. Not Henry. The last thing anyone needed was the outgoing billionaire bursting onto the scene with his meaningful intentions with Brynn's mother arriving. The reunion with Coach would be difficult enough.

"I'm fine," Ry continued, eager to convince Brett everything was fine and Henry's presence wasn't required. "Brynn is a teammate. A...friend."

Saying *friend* left a funny taste in Ry's mouth even though that was what they were. Okay, he liked her. He might be a little more concerned about her than other friends, but she'd been through so much. She also had no one but him right now.

Readjusting the phone against his ear, he stared at the bed.

At Brynn.

"Henry made her sound like more than a friend," Brett said in a matter-of-fact tone.

"I hadn't really talked to her until a few days ago." That much was true.

No one needed to know about the night they'd slept in the same hotel room. Or the hot kisses they'd shared here in Sun Valley. Or how much he enjoyed being with her.

Whatever was happening between them was temporary. He wasn't looking for a date, let alone a girlfriend. *Except...*

That hadn't stopped Ry from wanting Brynn to be in Portland. He'd justified asking Henry about his guest house so she wouldn't have to pay rent and would have nearby skiing. The fact Ry lived there, too, hadn't been the reason he wanted this. He was trying to do what was best for her.

"Brynn's had a rough season," Ry added. "That's

why our coach asked me to help her. She may find herself homeless soon so that's why I reached out to Henry."

"You sure aren't the same Ry-Guy you used to be." Brett sounded surprised. "First you detour your flight to help Cara in the Bay Area, and a couple of weeks later you're in Sun Valley helping Brynn. You're making the rest of us look bad."

"Just doing what I can." So many had stepped up to help him recover, especially Brett and Henry. That was why Ry was happy when his two friends had asked if he could pick up Cara O'Neal, an employee at their favorite bookstore in San Francisco who'd found herself in the middle of a Hollywood scandal, and fly her to Portland. Saying anything other than yes hadn't entered his mind. The same when Coach asked him to come to Sun Valley. Ry didn't want to be known as the arrogant, self-centered skier he'd once been. "And I even got to attend Cara and Brody Simmons's wedding."

"Laurel loved the photographs you sent."

"Thought she might, since Brody is her favorite actor. So are we good now?"

Brett laughed. "Yeah, Henry's overreacting. He must have read more into your earlier call because you sound the same to me."

"I am the same." Other than Ry's concern over Brynn's injuries and if she'd be healed enough to compete on Sunday and how tomorrow would go when her mom arrived, he was the same as usual. He just had more on his mind, all of which revolved around Brynn. "Did you call off Henry?"

"I texted him." Brett sounded like he was smiling. "Invited him to tuck in his goddaughter tonight to make up for you not needing him."

Ry blew out a breath. "Thank you."

"If you need—"

"I know who to call." But the only thing he needed was in this room—Brynn. "Tell Henry thanks. I'm flying home on Monday, and I'll give you both a call."

"Good luck helping Brynn."

"Appreciate that." Except luck might not be enough.

As Ry approached her bed, he had a feeling Brynn would need a miracle to get through the next few days. He hoped she got one.

Chapter Thirteen

The next morning, Brynn was sore and stiff. Natural light filled the room. Much nicer than the darkness that surrounded her when a nurse had woken her up in the middle of the night to take vitals. The chair where Ry had slept last night was empty.

She swallowed a sigh. No reason to be disappointed. He'd stayed the night when he could have stayed at the condo with a comfortable bed.

The door to her room opened. Ry entered, holding two cups of coffee.

Her breath caught in her throat. Tingles flowed

through her. He wore the same clothes as yesterday. Even with his hair a mess, he was still gorgeous. She swallowed. "You're still here."

"Good morning." He greeted her with a grin. "I thought you could use one of these."

"Exactly what I need to get going this morning." *Next to him.*

"Two sugars and a dash of cream." He handed her a cup. "Your face has more color. Feel better?"

"I do." Once she got moving, her muscles would loosen. "Doctor Wu wants me to walk the hallways."

"After you finish your coffee, we can take a stroll." Ry stretched. "I could use some exercise."

"You didn't have to sleep in the chair."

"Yes, I did." He winked. "I wasn't about to tempt Coach's wrath by sharing your bed again."

Too bad, because she'd enjoyed falling asleep next to him during her nap. His warmth and strength had made her feel safe and accepted, something that had been eluding her lately. She had no idea if the feelings were due to her situation, injury, or Ry himself, but she didn't need to analyze them when he'd been upfront about not being interested in dating or relationships. But that wasn't stopping a crush from developing. *Not that he'd ever know.*

She grinned. "That's interesting, considering you used to be the one who stood up to him."

"I still do with Coach, but not the man who suddenly found himself a father."

Her lips parted. "He's not. I mean, he is biologically. But he didn't seem to want—"

"This situation is new to both of you." Ry ran his hand lightly along her right arm. "It's taken twenty-five years for the truth to come out. Don't expect everything to be resolved right away."

For all she knew, it would take another twenty-five years for any resolution. Still, she nodded.

"But, I have a feeling you're in for a pleasant surprise," he added.

If only... But she didn't dare let herself believe it. Not yet. She sipped her coffee.

Her silence didn't keep his face from brightening. "And when that happens, I'll happily say I told you so."

Funny, but he sounded as if they would stay in touch after they left Sun Valley. That was unexpected, but Brynn hoped they did. "If it happens, I doubt I'll mind you saying that."

He raised his cup in a cheer to her before taking a sip.

She enjoyed her coffee. "I want to change before taking a walk."

"Me, too." He set his coffee on her bed tray and then picked up his cinch sack. "I'll change in the bathroom, then you can have it."

The door closed behind him. Brynn couldn't believe how easy being around Ry was considering how they'd started out. She had no idea how to define what was going on between them. She enjoyed spending time with him and kissing him. Beyond that...

The bathroom door opened. He came out and struck a pose. The striped jogger pants combined with the long-sleeved T-shirt resembled an American flag. "What do you think?"

"Only you could pull that off." Smiling, Brynn took a picture on her cell phone. "Chas, Sam, and Jon must have had fun packing for you."

"They're probably still laughing. Though these clothes have to belong to someone." As Ry moved toward the bed, he motioned to the bathroom. "Your turn."

Cautiously, she slid off the bed.

He held out his arms to spot her.

"I'm okay." The slipper socks the hospital provided kept her from sliding, but each movement sent a burst of pain shooting through her. Nothing Brynn couldn't handle if she wanted to ski on Sunday. "But thanks for watching out for me."

He grabbed her cinch sack. "Do you need the nurse to help you dress?"

"You're not offering?" she teased.

"That's what old Ry would have done." He raised an eyebrow. "Though if you ask..."

With a laugh, she took the bag. "I can do this myself."

Brynn could, but once inside the bathroom, she

left the door unlocked. She might be determined to do this, but she wasn't stupid. If she fell or the pain got too bad, she would need help.

After untying the straps, the gown came off easily. Dark bruises covered her left side. Not pretty, but they would heal. Not by Sunday, but she would do the best she could to finish the race. A little hurting wouldn't stop her.

Wiggling into her panties while standing proved too challenging, so she sat on the toilet. That helped. One attempt at putting on her bra made her shove the thing into the bag. The clothes Amelia had packed were baggy enough no one would notice. If they did, Brynn didn't care. After a quick check in the mirror followed by a grimace, she left the bathroom.

Ry gave her the once-over. "You look nice and comfy."

"Comfy, yes, but not so nice." She wore loose-fitting sweatpants and an oversized thick shirt. "I prefer yoga pants, but Amelia made the right choice. Anything formfitting would hurt the bruises."

His mouth slanted. "What about your racing suit?"

"I'll be better by Sunday." Brynn crossed her fingers behind her back. She had to be. "Ready?"

"Always ready for you."

Her heart bumped. It had been doing that a lot with Ry. Not surprising given all he'd done for her. "Be careful or I might take you up on that."

"I'm all yours until Monday morning."

With that, an imaginary bucket of ice water was dumped over her head. Monday he returned to Portland for his physical therapy, conditioning, and modeling. And she...

Stop.

Real life would intrude soon enough. No sneak preview required. She needed to focus on healing and enjoy this time with him because that was all she would get.

She held out her hand. "Ready to catch me if I fall?"

Ry laced his fingers with hers. "I've got you."

For now.

If only he didn't have to let go...

Slowly, they left the room and went into the hall. Each step hurt, but not to the point of grimacing. That was progress. She didn't want anyone, including Ry, to think she wasn't capable of competing in the giant slalom. But after the third lap, she needed a break. "Time to ice."

He gave a mock bow. "Whatever you wish."

"I wish you'd go to the course and text me updates. Not knowing what's happening is driving me crazy." She entered her room. "Please."

"You're not getting rid of me." His voice was calm and steady, but he had to be bored. "Text Taylor for updates."

"You hate hospitals."

Ry shrugged. "Staying."

Brynn blew out a breath. "If you're still trying to make amends—"

"You forgave me. I want to be here." He appeared genuine, which warmed her heart. "After lunch, you'll likely be discharged. Someone needs to drive you to Sun Valley. It might as well be me."

"Thanks." His choosing to stay pleased Brynn. Her growing attachment—dare she say affection— didn't scare her as much as it should.

Friends, teammates, and...

Brynn brainstormed a list of nouns to fill in the blank.

Crush, Date, Boyfriend.

Others came to mind, but those were nothing but fantasies and daydreams. She wasn't about to list them. Even boyfriend was pushing it, given what Ry had told her.

A date, however, would do nicely.

Brynn hoped Ry would be up for one after she finished racing and before he returned to Portland. After that, they could finish their evening with cookie dough and kisses.

Friday after lunch, while Ry went to find the doctor, Brynn hung up from talking to her brother Ace who had called before his game. As she sat on the bed staring out the window, she daydreamed about skiing. Not racing, but with Ry, making fresh tracks in knee-deep powder, switching off the lead, until they skied side by side. *Someday...?*

Probably not, but thinking about that was easier than imagining her teammates and coaches at the slalom course. Brynn wanted to be there, but she was stuck in the hospital.

Only for one night, and that was frustrating enough. This, however, gave her a glimpse of what not competing, let alone skiing, must be like for Ry. Yet, he'd pushed past those emotions to come to Sun Valley to help her, to stay with her at the hospital.

Could that mean something more than him being a teammate helping another? Or a friend?

She hoped so.

Possibilities ran through her mind. Ry didn't want a relationship, but that didn't mean they couldn't see each other, text, talk, or video chat. Friends did that. And no big deal if they happened to kiss occasionally. Friends did that, too.

Being around Ry made her feel as light as the mylar balloon floating in the corner of the room. After three months with an elephant pressing against her shoulders and chest, she wasn't ready for that feeling to end.

A text notification sounded.

Jax: *How's my fave skier?*

Brynn: *Ready to be free from her cage.*
Jax: *Don't push yourself.*
Brynn: *When have I done that?*
Jax: *Since you started crawling.*
Brynn: *Like you'd remember that.*
Jax: *Bet you're smiling.*
Brynn: *Maybe but you should score a goal for me tonight.*
Jax: *I play defense.*
Brynn: *So?*
Jax: *I'll see what I can do.*

Dr. Pearl entered the room.

"Good news." Dr. Pearl smiled. "The MRI results are unremarkable. Everything is normal, so you're going to be released. Coach Tolliver wants you to rest. No going to today's events."

"Will do, doc. I won't leave my room." Anticipation flowing through her, Brynn leaned forward. "What about racing on Sunday?"

"You'll need to speak with Dr. Wu and the coaches." Dr. Pearl gave her a conspiratorial wink. "But if you're up for skiing, fight for it."

Brynn wanted to race in the super G. She was ready to wage an all-out war with the coaches, if need be.

"I'll have the nurse arrange for your discharge," Dr. Pearl added. "I want you in bed until then."

Brynn covered herself with the blanket and held the stuffed husky. "Whatever you say."

Dr. Pearl laughed. "Good luck."

"Thanks." Though Brynn hoped she didn't need it.

After the doctor left, Ry came into the room. "I hear you're getting out of here."

"Soon, but I'm supposed to rest until then." His face appeared flushed as if he'd been running, but he didn't seem out of breath. "Where have you been?"

"After I spoke to the doctor, I ran an errand. So, naptime?"

She yawned. "I'm a little tired."

He kicked off his shoes and hopped on the right side of the bed. "Human pillow at your service."

Brynn wouldn't be complaining about having to rest now. She scooted over to give him more room. "I'm getting spoiled."

"You deserve it."

She peered through her eyelashes. "I do."

Laughing, he placed his arm around her, avoiding her left side as much as he could. "Come closer."

She didn't have to be told twice and cuddled against him. The sound of his heartbeat against her ear soothed her. His body heat warmed her. His touch offered a sense of belonging she hadn't thought possible. Not with so much else going on.

"Sleep," he murmured.

By the time Brynn woke up, it was time for her to leave the hospital. She signed the paperwork and received instructions to follow. As she sat in a wheelchair with the stuffed dog on her lap, a nurse pushed her to the curb where a four-door sedan idled.

Ry jumped out of the driver's seat, hurried around the front of the car, and opened the passenger door. "That didn't take long."

As he helped her, Brynn slid into the car. She fastened her seat belt.

"We have one stop to make," he said.

"Where?"

"You'll see."

Her lower lip thrust forward. Guess he wasn't going to tell her.

A short time later, they were in Sun Valley, parking in front of a lovely mountain lodge-style hotel that would have fit perfectly in a quaint European mountain village. Animal sculptures flanked each side of the entrance.

He turned off the car. "Let's go inside."

Her breath caught in her throat. The picturesque inn seemed like the kind of place a couple might escape to for a romantic getaway. They'd been getting closer since her fall, but she hadn't expected him to do this. Whatever *this* might be.

Brynn's pulse raced. "What are you up to?"

He didn't answer, but he got out of the car and opened her door.

"Such manners." She slid out, forcing herself not to grimace or flinch from the pain. Moving continued to hurt. Her fingers dug into the stuffed dog she carried to keep from crying out.

Ry carried her cinch sack, the flowers, and balloon. "Follow me."

She hesitated. "I'm not big on surprises."

"Who said anything about a surprise?"

He hadn't, except… "Then why are we here?"

Mischief twinkled in his eyes. "You'll see in a minute."

Inside, traditional-style furnishings filled the lobby. Old-world charm mixed with stylish mountain warmth. The fabric patterns and textures combined with polished wood reminded her of Europe.

The place was empty except for the hotel staff, and then she remembered the race and the ski resort. Why would anyone be inside when they could be out on the mountain? Well, unless they were with a hottie skier. She'd much rather be here than standing out in the cold unable to compete. Was Ry thinking the same thing?

Her heart rate sped up as if she were making quick turns through blue and red poles on a slalom course. "Has it been a minute yet?"

"Patience."

Brynn was trying, but her bruises hurt and an ache inside—one that had nothing to do with her injuries and everything to do with Ry's kisses—grew.

A woman with sandy blond hair stood by the elevator. Brynn did a double take. "Mom?"

"Surprise!" her mother shouted.

Brynn gaped. She touched her lips. "You...you told me you weren't coming."

"Oh, sweetie." Her mother hugged her lightly. "I had to come after Ry called me."

Brynn had told him why her mom wouldn't be here, yet... "You called my mom? Even after I told you...?"

No regret shone in his gaze. "You need your mom here, and that's what I told her."

"It's true, and he bought me the plane ticket," her mom confirmed. "Even though I should have realized that for myself."

Brynn should be upset at him, but instead she tingled all over. How could she be angry when he understood what she needed? Ry had stepped up in a big way when he could have done nothing. His actions and generosity touched her. "Thanks."

"We'll talk later. Rest now." He handed over Brynn's cinch sack, the flowers, and balloon. "You're staying with your mom tonight. Coach Tolliver and Dr. Wu agreed."

"I'll take good care of you," her mom said.

"Tomorrow, if you're ready, you can move back to your room with Lila." With his finger, Ry caressed Brynn's cheek.

So gentle. She wanted to thank him but couldn't find her voice. Not with her throat thickening with emotion.

"You've got my number," he continued. "I'll be

back in the morning."

He pressed his mouth against hers. Tender and soft. His kiss surprised Brynn, but she loved the feel and taste of him. Warm with a hint of salt, unmistakably Ry.

He stepped away. "Enjoy this time with your mom."

As he headed through the lobby, her mom's gaze bounced from Ry's retreating figure to Brynn. "You haven't mentioned him. Is it serious?"

"No." A part of Brynn wished it were because Ryland Guyer was everything she never knew she wanted in a man. "The coaches asked Ry to help me. That's why he's here."

The elevator doors opened. Laughing, her mom stepped inside. "Some help."

Brynn followed, and her cheeks warmed. "Mom."

"He seems to take his job seriously. He also kissed you."

The elevator doors closed.

"We're not together, not even close. That kiss…" Whatever Brynn said would only raise more questions. Ones she didn't want to answer. "Until this week, we didn't really know each other."

"That doesn't seem to be the case now." Concern clouded her mom's gaze. "Please be careful. Male elite skiers are only concerned with one thing…themselves. They will put their skiing first each and every time. You've been through enough.

You don't need your heart broken, too."

It already had been by her mom and Sully. "Is that what happened to you and Coach?"

The elevator doors parted. Her mom motioned to a door on the left. "Let's talk inside."

Less than a minute later, they stepped into the room. The mauve and cream color scheme contained a combination of plaid, stripes, and geometric-patterned fabrics. Oak furniture with a French flair didn't take away from the open feel of the room. A nightstand separated two queen-sized beds. A table with two upholstered chairs occupied a corner, and a cabinet held a flat screen television. "Lovely room."

"Ry booked it for us."

Of course he did. His errand must have been taking care of her mom's arrival. The realization sent tingles skittering across Brynn's skin.

"You have goose bumps." Her mom sat on the bed farthest from Brynn.

The good kind, but Brynn wanted to keep that to herself. She climbed under the covers of the bed closest to her. "I'll be warm soon enough."

The lines on her mother's face appeared deeper, but she still looked to be in her forties, not late fifties. A hair stylist took care of the gray in her hair. Running after four grandchildren kept her active and in good shape.

Brynn wished her mom had sat on the same bed with her. "You were going to tell me what happened."

"It's nothing, really. Just a warning."

"Because of your experience with Coach?"

Her mom nodded. "I was so young. We both were. When Mike…Coach Frederick…made the national team, he was so excited. I didn't blame him. It was everyone's dream. He wanted to make the most of the opportunity. A girlfriend back home would have been a distraction. So he broke up with me. I never saw or heard from him again until the wedding."

Not "nothing." The pain underlying what she said was clear. Coach Frederick had broken her mom's heart.

Brynn reached across the space between the beds to touch her mom's knee. "I'm sorry."

"That was a long time ago, but I remember what it was like. Please be careful around Ry. Anyone who follows skiing knows he's set on competing in Beijing."

Not only competing. Winning. And like Coach, Ry wanted nothing to distract him from his goal. That included women.

Her.

She pulled back her arm and adjusted the pillows behind her.

"Are you thirsty?" her mom asked. "Ry filled the fridge with food and drinks."

"I'm fine." Brynn rested against the headboard. "I'm happy you're here."

"Me, too. Though it shouldn't have taken a call from Ry to get me on a plane. Sully…" Her mom exhaled before wiping her eyes. "I'm sorry for what I've put you through. I had no idea what the consequences of my actions would be to you. Now, or back then."

It's okay sat on the tip of Brynn's tongue. Only she realized what happened wasn't okay. She remembered what Ry had said last night. "You had your reasons."

"Not very good ones given the way Sully treated you. I grabbed the stable and secure life instead of following my heart and taking a risk. I assumed when he agreed to give you his name he would accept you as his daughter. But he never even tried. My decision was the right choice for your brothers but not for you. I allowed Sully to treat you horribly. I was too afraid to speak up. Worried what might happen to you, your brothers, and me if I did. That was wrong, and I'm sorry."

Brynn had held a grudge against Ry. Avoided him as much as possible. Not spoken to him when he was near. Her anger had accomplished nothing except to build bitterness. The past belonged behind her; what had happened wasn't part of her present or future.

"I know you're sorry, Mom."

Her mother's expression grew more serious. "There's something you should know. When I told Sully I was flying to Sun Valley to see you, he gave me an ultimatum—you or him. I chose you."

Brynn gasped. Sully's actions didn't surprise her, but she was shocked her mother had gone against him. Her mother, who needed stability and was so dependent on her husband, had thrown her safe life—and the family—into upheaval. "What will you do?"

"That's a conversation for another time. Today is about you."

"Mo–om."

"Brynn."

"Thanks for coming." Brynn felt as if she were in the middle of a dream. That was a hundred times better than the nightmare she'd been living these past three months. "Having you here…"

"I'm relieved Ry called and kept me from taking the easy way out once again." Her mom sighed. "There's no place else I'd rather be. I hope you believe that."

Unfamiliar peace settled around Brynn's heart. "I do."

She would have to find a special way to thank Ry for getting her mom to Sun Valley. This was exactly what Brynn needed.

Maybe Sunday after the race…

Chapter Fourteen

That evening, Ry attended the concert, one of the many events put on in conjunction with the racing. The music had people on their feet dancing, but he couldn't stop thinking about Brynn. He hoped things were going well with her mom and her recovery because she'd been moving slow at the hotel. He kept checking his cell phone to see if she needed something.

No texts or calls arrived. That should have been a good sign, except not hearing from her made him miss her more. He wasn't used to missing anyone.

Well, except their family dog, Cocoa.

"Hear from Brynn?" Taylor asked.

He shoved his phone in his pocket. "No. Brynn's with her mom."

Sam snickered. "If she was that into you, she'd be texting. Mom or not."

"Brynn's injured." Chas stood behind Taylor and pulled her against his chest. "She's probably asleep because of the pain meds."

Ry appreciated Chas's input because that would explain why Brynn hadn't texted him. Not that he would contact her when she needed this time with her mother. His friends, however, weren't making it easy to get his mind off her.

Not surprising.

Brynn Windham was different from other women he'd met. She could be stubborn and a hard-nose, as she'd been on Monday, but being with her brought a welcome and unexpected peace. Something that had eluded him for…as long as he remembered.

A relationship was the last thing he wanted, but he wasn't ready to put distance between them. Monday would come soon enough. Until then, he wanted to spend as much time with her as he could. That gave him an idea—something he could do for her tomorrow night to help her forget all her troubles so she would be ready to race the next day.

On Saturday morning, Ry couldn't wait to see Brynn. He'd made plans last night when he returned to the condo. Now, he couldn't wait to surprise her. He only wished another week of races remained so he wouldn't have to say goodbye to Brynn and fly home. Though if he could convince her to come with him…

Two hours later, Ry watched the parallel slalom races, but by the second one he gave up trying to appear interested and headed over to the hotel instead.

After he knocked on the door, Mrs. Windham motioned him into the room. "I can't thank you enough for all you've done for me and my daughter. You've been a good friend to Brynn."

He bristled. Was *a good friend* how Brynn described him? He hoped not, after her mom had witnessed the not-exactly-friends kiss, but he couldn't shake his unease. Okay, they were friends, so he didn't know why that made him squirm.

Ry, however, kept smiling. "Happy to help, Mrs. Windham."

"Please, call me Deanna."

He didn't see Brynn in the room. "Where's…"

The bathroom door opened, and Brynn stepped out, wearing sweatpants and a hoodie. These weren't as baggie as what she'd worn yesterday. Someone must have brought her more clothes, ones that fit better.

Her face brightened, making her even prettier. "You're here."

Ry gave a mock bow. "At your service."

"See." Brynn grinned at her mom. "I told you he was here to help."

A hesitant smile appeared on her mom's face. "You did."

She moved to the opposite side of the room as if to give them privacy. That wasn't enough distance when all he wanted to do was hold Brynn in his arms and kiss her—an unfriend-like reaction.

Brynn's gaze narrowed. "Have something you want to say?"

He had lots to tell her, starting with *you're so beautiful* and ending with *we're more than friends.*

His heart lurched. He couldn't say any of those things to Brynn. He'd meant it when he told Brynn he wasn't interested in dating. So why was this craziness popping into his head? Maybe he hadn't slept as well as he thought and was tired.

Ry picked up her cinch sack. "Let's get you to the team hotel. People want to see you. Some of the team parents want to meet your mom. And I have a surprise for you."

She stiffened. "You know I'm not—"

"Big on surprises," he finished for her. "I know, but you'll enjoy this one."

Through lunch, Ry kept his distance from Brynn. He did the same thing when he drove her to the team hotel. As the hours passed in her room with people coming and going, Ry focused on being patient.

He understood Brynn's teammates wanted to

spend time with her. Her mom's sideways glances suggested she was leery of him. Coach, who hadn't said much as if trying to avoid a public scene with Deanna, watched Ry's every move as if waiting for him to do something wrong.

Ry wouldn't. He pasted on a smile, sat in the chair at the table, and waited for the time he could be alone with Brynn. He'd arranged a special dinner to keep her relaxed, so she would be ready for the race tomorrow, if they allowed her to compete.

The final group of visitors, three young skiers from the D team, left. He sent a text they would be on their way to dinner shortly. He had no doubt a smug smile was on his face because everything was working out as he'd planned.

As the door closed, Brynn stretched out on her bed and wiggled her sock-covered toes. "That's the last of the visitors."

She'd chatted with everyone coming in and out of her room this afternoon, even when she had to be hurting. "Tired?"

"No." Brynn picked up her glass of water and drank. "I've been lying down since Thursday and I've rested enough. I'm ready to get up and move."

That was his cue to get the evening started. Ry approached the side of the bed with purposeful steps. "It's time for your surprise."

They wouldn't have long until she had to return—Coach Tolliver had given him an hour and a half—but ninety minutes was better than nothing. Brynn needed a special treat. So did Ry.

Her face lit up. "Cookie dough."

"Something better."

Her mouth slanted as if she were contemplating what it could be. "You're setting a high bar, but if the surprise means I get out of this room for a few minutes, you're my new best friend."

"It does. And I guess I am." Ry enjoyed joking around with her. Brynn's races so far might not have gone as she'd hoped, but she seemed more at ease than she'd been on Monday morning. "My birthday is September fifth. A BFF should know that."

"I'll mark the date down in my calendar."

He held out his arm to her. She hadn't complained once about her injuries, but she had made an occasional wince or grimace. "Let's go."

She laced her fingers with his. "I need shoes."

"Your fuzzy socks are fine." Ry helped her stand, but he didn't let go of her hand. He didn't want her to stumble or fall, but he also enjoyed touching her. "We're not leaving the hotel."

"You have me curious."

"Then my evil plan is working." He wagged his eyebrows.

She laughed, a melodic sound that seemed to spread through his entire body.

The hallway outside her room was empty. Good, because Ry didn't want to have to explain what they were doing or tell someone they couldn't tag along. He didn't want to share her tonight. They entered the elevator, and he pressed the button for the second floor.

"Do I get a hint?" she asked.

"No, because I don't want to ruin the surprise."

She blew out a breath. "This better be good."

He bit back a laugh. "Would your BFF let you down?"

Her mouth slanted. "I need to see my surprise before I answer that."

"Spoilsport," Ry teased. They exited the elevator and went a few steps before he stopped in front of a door, released her hand, and pulled out a key card.

Her forehead crinkled. "You have a room here?"

"Not exactly." After he inserted the card, the green LED lit. He opened the door to see the lights were on—well, dimmed—as he requested. Soft instrumental music played, too. Brett's recommendation appeared to be spot on. Now if the rest of the evening could go as well...

His heart pounded with a sudden case of nerves because he wanted tonight to be perfect for Brynn. He wanted her to be relaxed and happy and...

She motioned to the doorway. "Are we going in?"

Too late to change his mind. He stepped out of the way so she could go first. "After you."

She entered the room, gasped, and covered her mouth with her hands.

He followed her inside, allowing the door to close automatically behind him.

A table for two, covered in a white linen tablecloth, complete with candles and a centerpiece with three red roses, awaited them. A napkin folded like a crown sat on the top plate.

"What is this?" She sounded stunned.

Good, that was the reaction he wanted. He'd mentioned not wanting anything to be over the top, and the caterer had taken Ry's requests to heart. "Dinner."

"I don't..." As she faced him, her eyes gleamed. She hugged him quickly before she stepped away. "No one has ever gone to this much trouble for me."

"It was no trouble." He pulled out a chair so she could sit. "After everything you've been through, I thought a quiet dinner for just the two of us would be nice for you."

As she studied the table, her smile kept widening. "This is...wonderful. More than I could have imagined."

Pleased, he sat in the chair opposite her. "Dinner will arrive shortly."

Brynn placed her napkin on her lap. "How did you manage this?"

"Last night, I asked my friend Brett, who owns the condo, for a recommendation. It only took a phone call and a follow-up one this morning."

The gratitude in her gaze nearly sent him toppling

backward. He had to look away to break the strong connection between them. His temperature rose. He grabbed his water glass and gulped, but that didn't cool him off.

"Thank you for making things better." She reached toward the roses in the vase before pulling her arm back. "This surprise is…incredible. Perfect."

Pride made him sit taller. "I'm here to help you. That's what BFFs do for one another."

"The position is all yours."

The door to the room opened. A server with bleached hair and dressed in black wheeled in a cart. "I'm Martin. We have four courses especially selected for your dining pleasure."

Giggling, she leaned forward over the table. "He sounds more like a butler than a waiter."

Heat radiated at the center of Ry's chest. He loved seeing her so lighthearted and happy.

Martin lit the candles on the table, filled their champagne flutes with sparkling cider, and placed the bottle into a silver bucket filled with ice. "I'll have your first course on the table next."

As Martin returned to his cart, Ry raised his flute. "A toast. To my new best friend. May she have the race of her dreams."

Staring at him, she tapped her glass against his. A chime hung in the air—one full of possibilities.

"I hope the same thing for you when you're on skis." She took a sip.

He did, too, wishing this could be the first of many toasts they shared.

Martin placed a bowl in front of each of them. "Pumpkin soup garnished with toasted baguette slices."

"I love pumpkin." She raised a spoonful of the soup and swallowed. "Delicious."

"In case you're wondering, I didn't do an internet search of your favorite foods." Looking up how she drank her coffee had been too stalker-like, so he hadn't wanted to do that again. "The caterer had told me his winter menu, and it sounded good."

"I wouldn't have minded if you did another search, but if you had, we'd be eating pizza or tacos."

He tried the soup, tasting a hint of nutmeg, cinnamon, and ginger. "Both would have been excellent choices."

The flames on the candles danced. She focused on the table with a hint of wonder on her face. "This is better."

His chest puffed. Ry wanted tonight to be special for Brynn, but being with her was making this an evening to remember for him. One he didn't want to end.

In between eating their soup and a salad with apple chunks, sliced beets, and chopped walnuts, they spoke about everything from favorite movies to bands. They shared stories like when she was mistaken for Jax's girlfriend and how much he enjoyed babysitting Brett and Laurel's daughter, Noelle, and couldn't wait to get her on skis. One topic flowed naturally to another. When their main course, filet mignon with mashed potatoes and glazed vegetables, arrived and they ate, they continued talking in between bites. Any silence was natural, not awkward.

Ry couldn't remember the last time he'd enjoyed a meal as much as this one.

A chocolate torte topped with whipped cream and fresh raspberries was the fourth and final course served.

She eyed the dessert with longing. "If I eat all this, I won't fit in my racing suit tomorrow."

"Have a bite or two," he urged. "Then take the rest to your room."

"If I do that, I'll eat it all."

"You could share," he suggested.

"Yes, but"—the tip of her pink tongue darted out and wet her lips—"I'm not sure I would."

"Being honest is a good trait to have." He tasted the cake. "I don't think I want to share if I have leftovers."

"Told ya." She ate a bite before sighing. "I've died and gone to Heaven."

Staring at her, Ry felt the same way. This was a dinner between two friends, but the romantic atmosphere made it feel more like a date. That should bother him more than it did.

To stop him from saying anything embarrassing, he shoved another forkful of cake in his mouth. He enjoyed the chocolate, but he would rather taste Brynn's kiss.

Ry stared over the rim of the flute. "What are your plans after the competition?"

"I'll fly to Park City and see what happens next. Though I'm sure what's coming." She sounded more resigned than upset.

"There's year-round skiing on Mount Hood."

She nodded. "Timberline was one of the official training sites for PyeongChang."

"It's near Portland. I learned to ski there."

Brynn wiped her mouth with a napkin. "Lucky you."

"You should come." The invitation burst out.

"To Portland?"

"Yes." Palms sweating, he felt as if he was asking a girl out for the first time. The reaction made no sense. He would try again. "My friend Henry has a guest house. It's empty, and you could stay for free while you figure things out. You'd have skiing nearby. I'm there, too."

Man, that sounded stupid aloud. Ry grabbed his water glass and finished what was left. He should have practiced what he wanted to say instead of blurting it out.

Her nose scrunched. "You wouldn't mind if I was in Portland?"

"I wouldn't have mentioned it if I would. And don't forget we're BFFs now."

She laughed, but it didn't sound natural.

Ry's stomach clenched. He'd gone about this all wrong, making things awkward between them, which was the last thing he wanted. "It was just an idea. You don't have to decide this weekend. I'm sure you have other choices."

Hope shined on her face. "Not really, so I appreciate the offer."

He wanted to kiss her troubles away. He wanted... "You could keep your spot on the team."

Amusement twinkled in her eyes. She half laughed. "I might have better luck buying a lottery ticket."

At least she hadn't lost her sense of humor.

"Never say never." He noticed her fork lay on the cake plate. "Finished?"

She nodded. "The dinner was mouthwateringly good, but I can't eat another bite."

Ry stood, went around the table to pull out Brynn's chair, and helped her stand.

"Thanks for tonight." She didn't let go of his hand.

Before he could say anything, she placed her lips against his. Soft, warm, chocolatey. The kiss was almost shy, which made him cherish it—Brynn—more. He allowed her to lead and forced himself not to touch her or press his mouth firmer against hers.

She drew the kiss to an end, still holding his hand. "A perfect end to a perfect evening."

There was so much he wanted to say about tonight and her coming to Portland, but this wasn't the time. Not with the final race tomorrow. Her mind needed to be focused on skiing, nothing else, especially him.

The coaches and doctors hadn't mentioned if Brynn could compete, but she acted as if racing was a done deal, so he would follow her lead.

They told Martin goodnight, and then Ry escorted Brynn to her room.

"Thanks again for tonight." She was radiant.

Standing outside her door, he kissed her, hard and fast. That was all he dared at the moment. She needed to rest, and he should leave her alone.

He hugged her before taking a step away from her. "I want you to do three things for tomorrow's race: Stay focused. Go fast. Finish strong."

She repeated the words to him. "How'd I do?"

"Perfect." Smiling, he touched the tip of her nose with his finger. "You've got this."

"I hope so." A grin flashed on her lovely face. "Might be better, if I say, yes, I do."

"Much better." He wanted her to exude confidence, the way she had earlier in the season when she'd been unstoppable. The women's giant slalom was her last race of the championships. This was her time to shine, to show the coaches she deserved a spot on the team. "Nothing will get in the way tomorrow."

"I have nothing to prove to anybody, except…myself." She crossed her fingers.

"You don't need that kind of luck." He thought about her bruises, her parents being together for the first time in over twenty-five years, and the giant slalom. "You've got this."

If anyone could succeed, Brynn could. He'd never met a woman like her. He wished they had more…time. Maybe if she agreed to come to Portland, they would.

Chapter Fifteen

Focus. Fast. Finish.

Not exactly what Ry had told Brynn last night after they'd kissed goodnight, but that had become her mantra. She touched her lips, a reminder of his kiss, of him. Her crush had exploded into something more. Each time she repeated or thought the words, Ry occupied a bigger piece of her heart. That wasn't a distraction; it was a comfort.

The mantra kept her going through her first run of the day. Brynn finished, which was a huge accomplishment given her injuries. Her time wasn't good enough. She needed to go faster and complete the course. Imagining Ry's smile calmed her nerves. She could do this.

Focus. Fast. Finish.

Riding the ski lift for her second run of the giant slalom, Brynn repeated the three words. The wind hit her. Snowflakes pricked her cheeks like tiny pins. She covered her face with a scarf and mouthed the mantra.

In the warming hut, Brynn muttered the three words again. Standing outside waiting to race, she repeated them again. She kept on her jacket and pants to stay warm.

Focus. Fast. Finish.

Wes rubbed Lila's arms and shoulders, and Coach Tolliver offered last-minute advice. Lila skied first.

You've got this.

Tingles erupted, followed by a rush of satisfaction. Confidence filled Brynn. Thanks to Ry. The old Ry-Guy might be gone, but the new Ry had brought back the old Brynn.

Confident.

Driven.

Fearless.

She wouldn't let secrets and setbacks stop her. No settling. Her brothers would freak when they learned about their parents' split. Part of her wanted to warn Jax and Ace—to tell them about her real father—but they needed to hear the story from their mother. Even though her problems weren't resolved, and wouldn't be for a while, she no longer would allow family secrets to haunt her on the slopes.

With Ry's help, she'd overcome what was holding her back. They worked well together. Brynn wished she could help him accomplish his goal of winning the gold in 2022. Maybe if she went to Portland she could, but that wasn't something to think about now.

She focused on her breathing and what she would be doing shortly.

"Ready?" Wes asked.

"Yes." Her voice was strong, matching the way she felt. "Lila, Regina, and Ella have the three fastest times. I'll catch them."

"You can do it."

Brynn nodded.

I've got this.

She did.

And she knew the reason—Ryland Guyer.

He'd rallied around Brynn and supported her as if she'd been a longtime friend, not just a teammate who had ignored and avoided him. For that, she'd be forever grateful.

Grateful for him not giving up on her. Grateful for him making her open up and trust him. Grateful for him treating her so special, like she was the only woman in the world.

Keeping the secret was no longer an issue. The weight was no longer hers to bear. Her mother and her father were watching this race. That had never happened before.

Brynn swung her arms and stomped her feet. The movement sent a slash of pain through her but kept the blood flowing so she stayed warm.

Focus. Fast. Finish.

She didn't want to let Ry down.

Or herself.

She reviewed the line she would take down the course, skiing the race in her mind.

"You're coming up, Windham," Coach Tolliver said.

Brynn removed her jacket and pants. Her bruises hurt, but this wouldn't take long.

"The course is in better shape this afternoon. The wind's died down. Mother Nature's on your side for this run."

She gave a nod and wiggled her shoulders, eager to race.

"Number twenty-eight," an official called.

Brynn stepped up to the starting gate. She breathed through her nose and exhaled through her mouth.

Beeps sounded.

Once. Twice.

And she was off.

♥ ♥ ♥

Ry stood at the bottom of the giant slalom course with Chas, Taylor, and Sam. Deanna Windham watched with the other team parents. His heart pounded as if he were on the course himself.

Brynn appeared on the big screen.

He grinned. "That's my girl."

Chas stood next to him. "Still not into her, huh?"

"Just being supportive."

He shook his head. "Taylor's right. Ry-Guy's found himself a girlfriend."

Ry enjoyed spending time with Brynn. Liked kissing her. He'd worried when she'd been hurt. Last night with her had been amazing. That didn't mean she was the one for him or vice versa. After what she'd been through with her family, she needed to be put first. He wasn't sure he could make her the priority she needed to be. Not with trying to make a comeback and compete at the highest level. "Dude—"

"Shhh." Taylor stood in front of them. "Watch the race."

"Great turn," Chas cheered. "Her skis are dialed in."

"She's having a fast run." Ry studied the windsock. Flat. No wind. "The conditions are perfect."

Taylor squealed. "Brynn's split is better than this

morning's."

This season, Brynn had nailed the tops of courses but ran into trouble on the bottom. He hoped not today.

"Looking good." Ry glanced at the clock. "She's got a shot at beating Ella's time."

"Regina's, too," Chas said.

Brynn skied into view, flying down the course with precision and control. Her perseverance and tenacity left him in awe.

"Wow." Taylor's one word summed up the run. "Brynn is back."

No kidding. Seeing her succeed filled him with satisfaction. He balled his hands as if that could make her go faster. "Go, baby."

As Brynn raced toward the finish line, the atmosphere electrified with cowbells and cheers. Flags waved.

Just a few more gates.

Ry couldn't breathe. He wanted Brynn to win more than he'd ever wanted to win himself. He'd never felt this way watching another skier. Was this because he wasn't competing? Or would he feel this way if he were?

Brynn crossed the finish line and threw her hands, poles still attached, in the air.

"Second place." Taylor jumped up and down. "Brynn's in second place behind Lila!"

"Brynn nailed it," Chas said.

Happiness flowed through Ry. He'd gotten Brynn back on track. But suddenly that wasn't enough. This felt…unfinished. Yet he wasn't in a position for more, was he?

Lila, who was in first place, hugged Brynn. The two roommates laughed. Coach gave Brynn a high five. A gold-medal smile formed on her face. She searched the crowd.

"She must be trying to find her mom," Ry said, unsure where Deanna was in the crowd.

"Brynn's looking for you," Taylor and Chas said at the same time.

Why? Brynn didn't need to share her moment with him. She should enjoy the attention and make the most of her placing on the podium.

"Don't appear so shocked." Chas laughed. "You stayed with her at the hospital, flew her mom in from the East Coast, and surprised her with a private dinner last night. Of course, she wants to celebrate with you. You also earned a ton of bonus points with the coaches for helping her."

Ry's throat constricted. He may have started out helping Brynn for the team and to redeem himself, but that wasn't why he'd stayed with her or asked her mom to come or invited Brynn to dinner. He'd done those things because seeing her happy pleased him. He wanted to do whatever he could to make sure her smile didn't disappear again.

He hadn't done that for another woman since

Pippa.

Had Henry been correct? Ry gulped.

Doubts assailed him. He'd kept his heart off-limits for a reason. It was one way to control something when everything else in his life seemed so random and up to chance. He'd succeeded until arriving in Sun Valley and meeting Brynn again. He hadn't been able to stop her from getting close. He hadn't wanted to.

Impenetrable?

With a smile, Brynn had demolished the carefully constructed wall around his heart.

The sparkle had returned in her eyes, and he'd played a part in that. A big part.

His heart pounded like a drum. Their days together replayed in his mind from handing her a coffee on Monday in the cafeteria to kissing in the hallway last night.

Good times. Okay, great ones with the possibility of more.

Except he wasn't ready for a future with her. Not the kind with him comprising one half of a couple. That was waiting for him after Beijing along with a job at Guyer Gear. A conversation that had played in his mind.

How about after the giant slalom on Sunday we can share some cookie dough and a few kisses?

Best invitation I've had in a long time.

Since you swore off women?

Women.

A weight pressed against his chest as if the entire team had piled on top of him. He'd told her that, yet he'd sent mixed messages. Ones he hadn't fully comprehended.

Doubts filled his mind about what he wanted from her.

Oh, man. He'd asked her to come to Portland. His blood ran cold.

Chas gave him a nudge. "Brynn's waiting for you."

Ignoring his uncertainty, Ry flashed her a thumbs-up sign.

Emotions swirled inside him like a tornado. His confusion, however, made zero sense.

Because...

Nothing had changed. Not really.

He knew what he wanted.

Since being injured, his goals had been driving him. He had three more years to go. He couldn't give up now.

Ry's chest tightened.

What was he doing thinking about Brynn as anything more than a friend? His plans didn't leave room for dating, let alone a serious girlfriend. He'd spent too much time putting himself back together after his injury and subsequent self-destruction. He couldn't afford the distraction of a relationship. If he got involved with Brynn, he was taking a chance of falling apart again if something went wrong, if she got hurt again, or left him the way Pippa had.

The thought of either of those things happening paralyzed him.

And that was a problem. A big one.

Nothing could stand in his way of winning a gold medal in Beijing.

Nothing.

Including…love.

Chapter Sixteen

At the award ceremony, Brynn stood on the podium with a second-place medal around her neck. She tingled from head to toe with happiness. The joy lessened the pain of her bruises. A silly grin had to be plastered on her face. She didn't care.

As a crowd gathered around, she searched for Ry. She wanted to thank him for his help. Just knowing he was here made this experience a thousand times better.

"I can't believe we came in first and second." Lila glowed from atop the podium. She shimmied her shoulders as if ready to break out in a dance.

Brynn didn't blame her. She would join in if she wasn't worried it would hurt too much. But bouncing at the knees felt okay. "Believe it."

Photographers snapped pictures. The three top finishers struck poses. People cheered.

Her mom stood in the crowd with her cell phone out in front of her as if taking videos or pictures. Coach was to Brynn's left with the rest of the staff, including Dr. Wu, who took a picture. Her teammates photobombed each other's selfies. Typical award ceremony.

Seeing everyone so happy left Brynn breathless. She didn't want this to end. As she relished the moment, laughter bubbled over. One thing was missing—Ry.

She scanned the crowd again. He had to be here, but where?

The ceremony ended with more hugs before she climbed down from the platform to be surrounded by media.

"Brynn." A female reporter from a skiing website stepped forward. "How does it feel to make such a strong comeback?"

"I'm thrilled to have placed in the giant slalom with my teammate Lila Raines." Brynn hadn't had much press coverage since December, other than negative reports, but she didn't miss a beat in answering. "I'm grateful to Dr. Daniel Wu and the entire team staff for taking such great care of me after my fall in the super G so I could race today."

You've got this.

And she did.

Because of Ry.

Her heart filled with love for him.

Love.

Oh, my. She'd fallen in love with him, fallen hard and fast in only a few days.

Love, not gratitude. Though she was grateful to him. This was so much more.

I love him.

The realization should scare her.

But it didn't.

She trusted him. He'd helped her focus, heal, and find her smile again.

How could she not fall in love with him?

But he doesn't want a relationship.

Yes, but they'd never expected to meet and connect the way they had. People changed their minds.

He had goals.

Brynn would never stand in the way of his dreams. She wanted to support him the way he had her. Together they were better, stronger, faster. She had no doubt about that.

Hope battled logic.

Point, counterpoint.

Brynn knew which she wanted to win. Ry leaving

Sun Valley didn't mean things had to end. He'd found her a place to live in Portland. That had to mean he wanted to spend more time with her.

Anticipation surged. She wanted to see where things could go with Ry away from the competition and the team.

Just the two of them.

In Portland.

After pulling out a second place today with all she'd been through since December, anything was possible. She believed that wholeheartedly.

Brynn answered more questions for reporters and posed for pictures with fans. As the crowd thinned, she saw Ry standing off to the side and hurried over to him.

"I've been wondering where you were." She wrapped her arms around him. Every part of her body was covered except her neck and face. Him, too, but his warmth still blanketed her. She brushed her lips across his. "I can't thank you enough for everything. But tonight, I'll try."

"About that…"

His tone was harsher than Brynn would have expected given the circumstances. She realized his arms weren't around her. He stood ramrod straight.

A shiver ran along her spine.

What was going on?

Confused, her muscles tensed, making her bruises hurt more. She stepped away from him. "About what?"

"I'm flying home in a couple of hours."

"Oh." The word burst out. "I thought you weren't leaving until Monday."

"Something came up." His gaze met hers before he stared off in the distance. "This will give you more time with your mom."

No apology for canceling tonight. No rain check. Nothing, but mentioning her mom. That didn't make sense. Had Brynn imagined the connection between them? Their kisses? His asking her to come to Portland?

No, she didn't think she had. Unless she was unconscious in the hospital, and the last three days had been a dream. Brynn blinked.

Ry was still standing there. Only this time, he wouldn't look at her.

Brynn took a breath, hoping to calm herself and not hunch like a hundred pounds had been added to each of her shoulders. That wouldn't be fair to Ry. He'd been behind her one hundred percent. She needed to be as supportive of his leaving, even if she didn't understand why.

"I'm sorry you have to leave early." Brynn waited for him to say *me, too*, but he didn't.

After holding her feelings in and ruining her season, she wasn't about to do that again. She couldn't let Ry leave without telling him how she felt. Even if he might not want to hear what she had to say.

I've sworn off women, remember?

Brynn doubted she would ever forget that, but nothing would stop her. After taking a breath to muster her courage, she exhaled slowly.

"You've come to mean a lot to me this week." She kept her tone steady, but her insides trembled. "Without you, I wouldn't be wearing this medal."

"That was all you up there."

"Thanks to your help." With a gloved hand, she touched the medal, a talisman of strength she hoped to draw from. "I know your focus is on recovering and training, but I'm looking forward to seeing you in Portland."

"You can stay at Henry's for however long you need, but I might not be around."

Wait, what? She clutched the medal. "Are you going to be traveling?"

"Maybe." His tone was evasive. "Who knows what will happen?"

She stared at him in disbelief, not recognizing the man in front of her.

He angled his shoulders away from her. "Well, I guess this is it."

It? Did he mean goodbye? "I don't understand what's happening. Last night…"

"I don't want a girlfriend." He spoke fast as if he couldn't hold back any longer. "Nothing personal."

"You told me that."

"Yes, but I may have led you to believe I wanted more with you when I don't."

Her heart banged so loudly she was sure everyone on the mountain could hear it. She forced herself to breathe before she passed out. "Does that mean you no longer want me in Portland?"

"You need a place to go."

Her heart sank to her feet. Splat. He didn't want her there. He was offering charity out of pity or maybe guilt over what happened five years ago even though she'd forgiven him.

Brynn wanted no part of that. She raised her chin. "Don't worry. I'll be fine."

"I'm sorry, but this is for the best."

"What?" she asked, her tone confused. "How is you doing a one-eighty from last night for the best?"

He shifted his weight from one boot to the other. "You deserve better than a guy like me who is only focused on himself. You need someone who can put you first. Make you his priority."

"No." She shook her head as if to emphasize the point. "You aren't allowed to make this about me when this decision is all about what *you* want. That's what my mom did. I'm not letting you do the same."

"You're right," he agreed finally. "I'm sorry."

She released the breath she'd been holding. "In case you didn't realize it, all those things you say I deserve, you did this week."

"Only because Coach Frederick asked me." Ry

stared past her as if she was invisible. "If it were up to me..."

What he said sliced into her like a knife, cutting deep.

"You're an amazing skier. A great kisser. Fun to hang out with, but I need to get back to my life," he continued. "I told you what I've been doing, what I want and don't want."

He had. "2022."

Ry repeated the year.

Still, Brynn didn't want to give up. She hadn't let herself imagine a wedding or children, but she could picture a future together. A wonderful future full of possibilities. "But that doesn't mean you can't have more."

"Skiing is all I need."

He didn't need her. No one did.

She wanted to cry, but she tried to remain calm.

"I would never get in the way of your skiing. The way you wouldn't with mine." She forced herself to continue. "You can deny it all you want, but there's something between us."

"A vacation romance, that's all."

No, I love you.

A mitten-sized lump burned in her throat. She swallowed around it. "We aren't on a vacation."

He blew out a breath. "I'm not trying to hurt you. Just being honest before I leave. Since I've been here, I forgot what I need to be doing for myself."

She didn't want to believe him. Ry had acted like he was into her. Cared for her. Wanted her. Everyone else had thought so, too.

"Okay, but are you being honest with yourself?" Her voice cracked, but she kept going. "This past week has been special. I felt it. So did you."

"We were caught up in the moment. Both of us for different reasons. It wasn't anything special."

Fighting the heartache threatening to overwhelm her, she stared down her nose. "You're lying."

He flinched. "Just being selfish. A character trait of mine. Some call it a flaw."

"You've done so much for me, but something happened between last night and today. You changed." She waited for him to disagree, but he didn't so she continued on. "The Ry I fell for is gone. The old Ry-Guy has returned in his place."

Ry stiffened. "He may have been here all along."

Brynn hated what that implied, but she couldn't pretend he hadn't said it. Her mom had been right to warn her about Ryland Guyer. "Then you're correct. I do deserve better. Good luck with your skiing."

Turning away, she let go of the medal.

Whatever they'd had was over before it began.

Her heart splintered. As sharp shards poked at her chest, she made her feet trudge forward.

One step. Two steps.

Up ahead, she made eye contact with Coach and forced a smile. At least the skill she'd perfected the past three months would come in handy today.

He waved. "They want to take a quick video for the team's Facebook page."

Brynn kept a smile on her face when all she wanted to do was cry, even if Ry didn't deserve her tears. "Sure."

"You skied a near-perfect run today. Very proud of you, Brynn." Affection filled his gaze. "And that's not just your coach talking."

"Thanks. That means everything to me." Tears, a mix of happy and sad ones, stung her eyes. "Given my performance this season, I don't want to put you or the other coaches in an awkward position because we're, um, related, when I don't deserve a discretion spot. I didn't earn one. I understand you have to do what's best for the team, and it's okay. No hard feelings."

The regret on his face confirmed the truth—she wouldn't be on the team when the nominations announcement was made. "I appreciate that, and I'm sorry."

Brynn kept her chin up. "Other skiers have made it back on the team. I'll keep training. I'm not giving up."

"You better not." His gaze locked on hers. "I can help you in the off-season."

Not trusting her voice, she nodded. If only things could have worked out like that with Ry…

Coach peered over her shoulder. "Where's Guyer

going?"

She cleared her throat. "Home to Portland."

Deep lines formed a V between Coach's eyebrows. "I thought you and he were—"

"Ry did what you asked." Brynn didn't want to talk about this or she might lose it. "He helped me regain my focus. Got me through the races. That's all he was here for."

Unless she counted filling her with hope, making her fall in love with him, and then breaking Brynn's heart by not wanting to see her again.

"Are you sure about that?" Coach sounded surprised.

She nodded. "Skiing is all he needs. Wants."

Not me.

His loss.

Thinking that, however true, didn't make her feel better. If anything, her heart hurt more.

"What do you want?" Coach asked.

"Someone who wants me."

"You've got that." Coach shoved his hands into his jacket pockets. "Your mom and I... We have things to work through, but we will. We're here for you. Never doubt that."

The words were a soothing balm, but only a momentary respite from her pain. She'd lost so much, but that was no one's fault but her own. Both with her spot on the team and Ry. "Thanks. I'll see you later."

"Team dinner," he reminded her.

Another nod, even though a big, boisterous dinner was the last place she wanted to be tonight. All the people she knew and loved would no longer be her teammates. And Ry…

Brynn blinked to keep the tears at bay. Forget going to the dinner. She could beg off because of her injuries. Besides, there was only one thing she wanted to eat tonight—cookie dough. Lots of it.

Eating her favorite treat wouldn't put the pieces of her heart together again. Unfortunately, Brynn wasn't sure what would. But she figured it couldn't hurt.

Chapter Seventeen

After leaving the course, Ry walked around, trying to clear his head. He made two loops, but the exercise didn't quiet the jumble of thoughts. He wondered if anything would. Time, perhaps?

On the way to the condo, he saw Coach Frederick talking to Brynn's mom. Both spoke with strong tones and regret. Painful expressions crossed their faces. The emotion was almost palpable.

They hugged.

The embrace, full of so much longing, overwhelmed Ry. He couldn't stop watching the pair and nearly crashed into a garbage can. Maybe Coach would get another chance with Deanna. That would be good for both of them.

And Brynn.

Doubts clawed at Ry, poking into his heart with talons. Being with Brynn, working together this week, was so much better than being on his own, but he couldn't lose sight of the prize.

Beijing.

A gold medal.

Nothing else mattered, right?

Stupid question because he knew the answer. That was why he was taking off tonight.

At the condo, he sent texts to Brett and Henry about returning to Portland a day early. Both had replied the two of them would pick up Ry from the airport and have a late dinner with him.

At least he wouldn't be alone tonight. But every other night and day after that...

Don't think about it.

Her.

This was what he wanted. No distractions.

He'd made the right choice for his skiing.

And himself.

Especially his heart.

As Ry carried his bags to the front door of his condo, his arms tensed and trembled as if he were carrying sandbags in the gym. He rolled his eyes before setting the luggage on the floor.

Being upset over Brynn was stupid. A few days together—a couple of kisses—meant nothing. No reason to feel torn up about saying goodbye.

It was his choice.

He'd been honest with her about what he wanted. She'd wanted…

The Ry I fell for is gone.

His stomach churned. Feeling nauseous had everything to do with not eating lunch. He would grab a snack before his flight.

Ry went through each room in the condo to make sure he hadn't forgotten anything. And then he remembered…the kitchen.

He threw away the food in the refrigerator and left the nonperishables in the cabinet for Brett and Laurel. That should be it. He was ready to go.

A knock sounded.

Brynn?

His heart jolted. He ran to the entryway and opened the door.

Chas stood there, wearing his team jacket, a pair of jeans, boots, and a baseball cap. "Hey."

Ry gripped the doorknob. "What are you doing here?"

"You called to say goodbye." Chas's lips pressed together in a thin line. "It sounded like you needed to talk."

Ry had met Chas at a race when they were teenagers. The two of them had grown up together, literally and figuratively, training and racing across the globe. They'd seen each other at the best and the worst of times, but Ry wasn't sure what to say.

"I…" He dragged his hand through his hair. "I'm going home."

Chas entered the condo. "Does this have anything to do with Brynn?"

Ry started to speak but then stopped himself. He tried again. "I need to go."

"That tells me you taking off has everything to do with her."

He didn't deny it.

Chas sat on the couch as if settling in for a long conversation. "What's going on?"

"I don't know."

"You think leaving will help you figure it out?"

A fair question. Ry shrugged.

"Taylor's with Brynn."

An image of Brynn formed in his mind. Her bright smile disappearing as hurt filled her eyes. He'd caused her pain, as much, maybe more, than her fall the other day.

For the best.

Once Brynn realized she would be better off with a man who could make her his priority, she would be fine.

She had to be.

"Are they out celebrating?" he asked.

Chas gave him a disgusted look. "Yeah, with

cookie dough and a box of tissues. Whatever you said to Brynn after the race destroyed her."

She should be out having fun after the race she had. Except…

I can't believe you didn't feel something between us this week. Something special. I sure did.

He had, too. But that didn't mean anything. It couldn't.

More invisible sandbags landed on his shoulders. He rubbed his face. "I didn't mean to hurt her."

"You still did."

"But we never… We weren't together. Not as a couple. Not really. I wanted to help her. I did help. As Coach asked."

"So this was about earning points with Frederick?"

"Some of what I did was for Coach and the team." Ry remembered the first day. Finding out what had really happened in that hotel room. Wanting to erase his guilt. Helping her also seemed the best way to pay forward the support he'd received after being injured. Only she hadn't been one of the reasons he'd wanted to help. Not at first. They'd been all about him.

"Stay away from Coach. He looks like he wants to punch you," Chas warned. "He's acting protective of Brynn. Not that I blame him."

"I'm a selfish jerk."

"You could add a few other colorful adjectives to

that and not come close to what the women are saying about you. So what are you going to do to make this right?"

"Nothing." Standing in one place wasn't helping, so Ry paced across the living room. "Brynn deserves better. She's been dealing with so much since December. I'm getting away from her before I cause more damage."

"Running away."

"Leaving early," Ry countered.

"There's another choice."

Ry glared at his friend. "Go shoot Cupid's arrow somewhere else. There is no other choice. Brynn and me... We aren't like you and Taylor. Together forever. Love of your life. Soulmates."

Chas shook his head. "You know this already?"

"I..."

"It took me years to figure out I was in love with Taylor." A vein pulsed in his neck. "Why would you think you'd know about Brynn in a week?"

"It doesn't matter." Ry's mind was a jumble. He didn't know what to think other than Brynn had meant something to him. "I have goals. Falling in love isn't one of them. I need to focus. I can't afford to be distracted."

Brynn would be a big one. Who was he kidding? She already was.

Compassion shone in Chas's gaze. "I know what skiing means to you, but here's the thing. It's not all or nothing. You don't have to do this on your own. Be alone. I'm finishing up my best season ever. Taylor's been a huge part of my success."

"You guys are different. Everyone knew you'd end up together."

"Given what I've seen this week, the same could be said about you and Brynn. You're good together."

A part of Ry wanted to agree, but he didn't dare. That would mean admitting he was wrong and making a mistake by leaving this way. His muscles bunched. "Helping her was easy. But I'm focused on my recovery and returning to the team. Skiing has to be my only priority, not a woman—"

"You'll learn how to make both work. I won't lie. Juggling everything can be rough, but I'm a better man because of Taylor, and my skiing has improved. You can't beat celebrating with the woman you love or commiserating with her when things go bad."

"You and Taylor have known each other forever. It's only been since Monday with Brynn."

"But in that time, I've never seen you so happy. That has to count for something."

No, it didn't. Ry had let his guard down, and Brynn had taken over his heart in a way no other woman had. Not even Pippa. That terrified him. "I've been happy in Sun Valley, but Brynn and me…it's nothing more than a vacation romance."

Chas's jaw jutted forward. "Are you sure that's all it is?"

Ry couldn't answer because he wasn't sure of anything right now. A vacation romance would be easier to get over than leaving behind the love of his life.

Way to be melodramatic, Ry-Guy.

"Before you board the plane," Chas continued. "Think about what made you happy this week and what next week will be like without that."

Brynn made Ry happy. Without her, he would be…

He shook the thoughts from his mind. She was better off without him.

"It's not the right time." Ry had to stay focused. "I'm doing what worked after Pippa left me. I focused on making the team for Sochi."

"You're revising history, dude." Chas laughed. "You partied like crazy with a revolving door of women in and out of your life."

Okay, maybe Ry had, but he hadn't been focused on one woman. He hadn't even remembered what happened that night with Brynn, but he'd redeemed himself. Only to let her think the worst of him this afternoon.

"You're no longer that same guy," Chas continued. "You haven't been since being injured."

Ry couldn't quite fill his lungs with air. He hated what he'd said to Brynn even if it had been for her own good, even if she hadn't believed him. One day she would understand.

"There isn't a set timeframe for relationships. I wish there was because Taylor and I wasted so much time, years, because I didn't want to mess up our friendship. Don't be stupid like me." Chas's face reddened, but Ry had a feeling the guy was angry at himself. "Don't let the time you've known Brynn be a factor. If you do, you could be throwing away something amazing."

I've been in love with Brynn's mother for nearly forty years.

Coach's words echoed in Ry's head. He didn't want to end up like Frederick and Brynn's mom. Ry didn't want to live with regrets. "I wish I could believe there's room for both Brynn and skiing."

"All you can do is give it a shot," Chas counseled. "You'll know soon enough if she affects your skiing. If not, it could be everything you never knew you needed."

"Speaking from experience?"

"Totally."

Ry's injury had taught him that life could change in an instant and that control was an illusion. Other than during a race, he hadn't put himself, or his heart, on the line. Not since Pippa. Years ago, he'd been hesitant because of his experience with her. But he hadn't moved on. Not really. He'd allowed that heartbreak, his own selfishness, and his fears to influence him. He hadn't realized that, however, until now.

Because of that, he'd hurt Brynn.

Lost her.

The Ry I fell for is gone.

He'd fallen for her, too.

Fallen hard and never had the chance to tell her before messing everything up.

Chas wasn't the stupid one. That honor belonged to Ry.

He had to do something. Beg for forgiveness. Ask for another chance.

It was probably too late, but so what? Ry couldn't be any worse off than he was right now. He had to try to fix this.

He'd already lost his heart. He didn't want to lose his future, too.

Chapter Eighteen

A plastic container of chocolate chip cookie dough sat on the bed next to a half-full box of tissues and the stuffed Siberian husky Brynn had received from Coach. A text notification sounded followed by a second one. She checked her cell phone.

Not Ry. Her brothers in a group text.

Jax: *I heard about your second-place finish. WTG!*
Ace: *Podium. You did it, B!*
Jax: *BTW, Mom told us everything. Sully is pissed, but what's new? Haven't talked to the others, but this changes*

nothing for Ace and me. You're the best baby sis ever. Love ya!
Ace: *Love you, B!*

Brynn's breath hitched. Tears welled. She hadn't known how much she needed to hear from Jax and Ace. She typed on her phone.

Brynn: *Thanks! Love you both. Will call tomorrow xoxox.*

Another text notification beeped.

Jax: *Call anytime. If you need us. Money. A place to stay. Whatever. We're here for you.*
Always.
Ace: *J has more money than me, but I have room for you.*
Jax: *I have lots more money and a guest room in a much nicer place than that pit Ace calls home. We all know who your favorite bro is.*
Ace: *That would be me. I'm also the hottest.*
Jax: *In your dreams.*
Ace: *You're just jealous because I have all my teeth.*

Brynn laughed. That felt good after crying so much. The relief at knowing—and seeing via their texts—nothing had changed with Ace and Jax made her breathe easier. She set her phone on the nightstand.

Spoon in hand, Taylor leaned against the bed's headboard. "Who are you texting?"

"Two of my brothers." Leaning forward, Brynn stuck her spoon into the remaining dough. No one knew about Coach being her father or what that meant to her family. He and her mom could decide if they would tell others or not. She'd seen them talking earlier. Brynn was fine with whatever they decided. "If I want to leave room for dinner, I'd better stop eating this."

"Everyone will understand if you want to bail tonight."

"The team, yes, but not my mom." Brynn inhaled slowly. Dinner would be the safest place to see her mother tonight. With others around, her mom wouldn't question her about Ry not being there. Brynn hoped he didn't even come up in conversation. "I can survive a meal without crying or falling apart."

Taylor frowned. "You should be celebrating, not surviving."

"I'll get there." Brynn eyed the cookie dough but didn't touch the spoon sticking out of the container. "Thanks for hanging out with me. I didn't want Lila to feel obligated to stay."

"I'm happy to be with you. I just wish things had turned out differently with Ry. I thought…" Taylor sighed.

"It's okay."

Maybe not at this moment, but it would be.

Once her heart had time to heal. That might happen sooner rather than later given her life was about to drastically change with losing her spot on the team and her family situation. Figuring out what she should do next would keep her from focusing too much on Ryland Guyer.

Besides, maybe he was right. Spending a week with a guy hadn't given her much time to get to know him. Her heartache and disappointment was genuine, as was her love for him, but everything else could have been wishful thinking on her part. She would never know now.

A knock sounded on Brynn's door. "Lila must have forgotten her key."

Not surprising, given her roommate had been so giddy since winning she'd misplaced her phone and her jacket. Twice. Brynn moved to the edge of the bed.

"Stay put." Taylor stood. "You must be sore."

Throbbing bruises were nothing compared to the way Brynn's heart hurt. "Thanks."

The door opened. "Hey, Chas. Ry…?"

Brynn's muscles bunched. *Ouch.* Doing that made everything hurt more. She grabbed the stuffed dog as if an inanimate object full of fluff could protect her.

Taylor glanced back with a contrite expression. "I—"

"You'll see Brynn at the team dinner." Chas grabbed Taylor's coat, held her hand, and pulled her toward him. "Time to go."

Taylor made the call-me sign with her hand, and

Brynn nodded. The couple left.

Ry stepped inside before closing the door behind him. He clutched his beanie in his hands. His sad expression, as if he'd lost a best friend, matched the way she felt. That was his fault, not hers.

Silence enveloped the room. He'd been the one to come to her, so Brynn would wait for him to talk. She clutched the husky tightly, holding it in front of her like a shield.

He took a step forward and then stopped. "You got your cookie dough."

Brynn didn't know what to say or do, so she grabbed a spoonful of cookie dough. She could have a salad for dinner if she had any appetite left by then. "Yes."

He shifted his weight between his feet. "I don't know how to begin, so I'll just say it. You were right."

"About?"

"Everything." He brushed his hand through his hair. "I was lying to you. To myself. I did feel something. But that was so unexpected, I reverted into jerk mode. I'm sorry for hurting you. That was the last thing I wanted to do."

At least Brynn hadn't imagined their connection. She released the breath she'd been holding. "Thanks for telling me. Apology accepted. Have a safe trip home."

Ry straightened. "I'm not leaving tonight."

Hope sparked, but reality extinguished it. "You

said…"

"I said a lot of things because I was confused. Being stupid. Scared. I was focused on the negative what-ifs instead of the positive ones." He took another two steps toward her. "I see the truth now."

"What truth?"

He rubbed his fingers over his hat. "I've fallen in love with you, Brynn. Head over heels, completely in love. That's the only thing that could explain my lashing out the way I did."

Air rushed from her lungs. Her pulse sped as if she'd just finished a race. Her stomach fluttered, not with butterflies but with hummingbirds. Hundreds of them. She forced herself to breathe.

Ry came closer. "You were brave enough to admit your feelings and say there's something special between us. It took me longer to find the courage that comes so naturally to you."

Brynn wanted to believe him, but she was afraid of being hurt again.

As he sat next to her on the bed, his thigh pressed against her right one. The touch jolted her like an electrical shock.

"I've screwed up twice with you now." He tossed his hat on the nightstand. "You deserve a better guy than me, but the thought of you with another man is enough to kill me. Please forgive me. Again. I don't want to lose you. If you can find it within your heart to give me another chance, I want to prove the adage the third time's a charm is true."

Her heart soared. Smiling, Brynn set the stuffed dog next to her. She didn't need protection. She needed to trust—him and herself. "I want you to prove that, too."

Ry was a caring, sweet man, who had freaked out today. Still, he'd brought out the best in her this week. Maybe she could bring out the best in him. She wanted the opportunity.

"You're here. You didn't leave. That tells me you want to make whatever this is between us work." Brynn clasped her hand in his. "But I have to be honest—how you acted earlier, what you said after the race, hurt me."

"I'll do whatever I can to make that up to you."

"I'll be bringing a lot of baggage with me. My parents. Sully. Brothers. A horrible season. It might not be as easy as it's been here."

"I don't care." He leaned into her. "We can overcome everything together. Get you where you need to be and not just with skiing. Same with me."

She squeezed his hand. "Together."

He nodded.

"I love you, Ry."

As his eyes widened, his lips parted. "You…"

"I love you," she repeated.

He touched her face as an expression of awe came over his. "I love you, too. So much."

The words wrapped around her like a hug, one she never wanted to end. Joy overflowed from her heart. "I could get used to you saying that."

"Me, too." Ry placed his hand on the back of her head and lowered his mouth to hers. His lips moved over hers with gentleness. A sweet kiss laced with longing. A loving kiss that hinted of a future together.

Eager for more, Brynn let go of his hand. She arched against him, deepening the kiss. This was how she'd wanted to thank him after the race—only this was oh-so-much better.

He pulled her closer, his touch light as if he remembered her injuries. Of course he did, and she carefully scooted closer until she was half on his lap. One hand splayed his back while the other wound in his hair. She would never get enough of him or his kisses.

As Ry pulled away slightly, affection filled his eyes. "We have plenty of time for this later."

Brynn swallowed a sigh. "My mom's expecting us. Me."

"Us sounds better." He ran his finger along her jawline. "But I have a feeling Coach will kill me."

She laughed. "Probably."

"But what a way to go."

"You'll have to face Ace and Jax, too."

"Just remind them I model." He brushed his lips over her hair. "Please say you'll come to Portland.

Move into Henry's guest house. I don't want us to be apart."

She wanted to scream "yes," but something held her back. "As long as you don't think I'll be in the way of your goals."

"You won't be. And we need new goals for both of us." He spoke fast. Not with nervousness but excitement. "You need to train, too. And I have another reason besides being together for wanting you with me."

She drew back slightly. "What?"

"Once I'm on skis, I'll need an awesome training partner to make me go faster. One who'll console me when I can't keep up. And one who'll forgive me when I screw up. Again." He brushed his lips across hers. "Know anyone who fits the bill?"

"I do, and she'll love Portland, though not as much as she loves you." Happiness filled her. "Are you willing to work hard to catch her?"

"I'll do whatever it takes and then some because I'm never letting her go. You're it for me." As he hugged her, the beating of his heart was strong and rapid like hers. "I love you, Brynn. Nothing will ever change that."

"I love you, too." Peace settled over her. She'd never expected to find love on the slopes, but that was exactly what had happened. And she had no doubt this was one race they would win. Together.

In May, Brynn's name wasn't on the list of alpine team nominations. The official team announcement would be made in November. She wasn't surprised, but she was still disappointed. Thankfully, Ry kept her smiling and skiing. Today, they skied on Mount Hood's Palmer Glacier. Nothing too intense since Ry was still getting used to being on skis, but the bluebird day was gorgeous. And, well, so was he. She couldn't ask for a better boyfriend.

Ry kept telling her that his folks loved her. His parents treated her more like a daughter than their son's girlfriend. His mom invited Brynn out for lunch and spa pedicures. His dad thought she'd fit right in at the company...if and when the time came. Whenever they did anything as a family, she was included. It hadn't taken long for Brynn to feel more like a Guyer than a Windham.

Ry had also introduced her to his friends in Portland. Not only was Henry Davenport's guest house nicer than the home she'd grown up in, but he treated her like a little sister. She had to keep telling him to stop buying her gifts, but she was coming to find that was just Henry and how he showed affection to those he cared about. Brett and Laurel Matthews had taken Brynn under their wing, giving her a part-time job for Laurel's interior design firm and inviting her over for dinner.

With Ry's recommendation and support, Brynn had been having weekly sessions with Doctor Dean and also seeing a local therapist to help with her family issues. She'd visited Jax and Ace before moving to Portland. As Sully had done, her three oldest brothers had cut off contact. Her mom had returned to Vermont. She'd been quiet about what she would do post-divorce, but she kept busy with her grandchildren, whom she was still allowed to see, and stayed in touch with Coach, as did Brynn. She couldn't believe how much had changed since March.

Ry had stopped ahead of her and stepped out of his skis.

Worry flashed through her. She skied to him. "You okay?"

He raised his face to the sun. "Just enjoying this beautiful day with my gorgeous girl."

"I thought something was wrong." Relieved, she laughed. "What am I going to do with you?"

He dropped to his left knee—the uninjured one. "Marry me, Brynn. I know we haven't been together long, but when it's right, you know. Make me the happiest man alive by agreeing to be my wife."

She blinked. Let what he'd said sink in. "You want to…"

Ry pulled out a ring box from his pocket. He opened it. A diamond solitaire gleamed against the black velvet. "I want to marry you."

"Yes. Yes." She forced air into her lungs. "I'll

marry you."

Brynn tugged off her ski gloves and then held out her left hand.

Ry put the ring on her finger. A perfect fit. "We're engaged."

"We're engaged." The future she'd been dreaming about was going to come true. "I love you."

"I love you." He kissed her on the lips. "This is only the beginning."

She held out her hand to see the ring better. "I can't imagine it getting any better."

A charming grin spread across his face. "Just wait."

Epilogue

The temperature in Beijing was chilly, but Ry's parka contained a built-in heating system to keep Team USA warm during the Opening Ceremony. The alpine team would be competing in Yanqing to the north, but no one wanted to miss tonight. Not if they wanted to experience all the Winter Games offered. He'd done this once before in Sochi, but it never got old.

Ry glanced around the staging area at the men

and women dressed in matching red, white, and blue winter apparel. Laughter and hugs from friends old and new in the staging area for Team USA added to the festive atmosphere, as did his gorgeous wife standing next to him and bouncing on the toes of her boots.

He stared at Brynn who wore a USA beanie. "You're so excited you can't keep still."

"Stop acting so chill," she teased. Her eyes brimmed with anticipation. Competing at the Winter Games was a dream come true for her, as it was for everyone waiting to march in the Parade of Nations, including him. "Being here means as much to you as it does me."

"It does." Ry's nerve endings tingled. Lowering his mouth to Brynn's, he stole a kiss that heated him from the inside out. He might not need the jacket to heat him. She could do that with a touch of her lips. "I'm just having fun watching *your* reactions."

Brynn nudged him with her shoulder. "That's fine, but please make sure you enjoy your own."

"I will." Staring at her, his heart filled with joy. Something that would happen whether here or at home in the States. "But you're glowing. It's impossible to take my eyes off you."

Her face brightened more. "I love you."

He would never tire of hearing or saying those three words. "I love you."

She wrapped her arms around him.

"Being here with you, both of us competing in the Games, I feel like I'm dreaming."

"Best dream ever."

Ry had believed nothing could match the intense emotions he'd felt marrying Brynn. His parents and hers—Coach and Deanna who were now married—didn't understand the rush to get married after being together for only a few months, but Ry knew Brynn was the one. He hadn't wanted to wait another day to start their life together; so on a sunny day at Timberline Lodge on Mount Hood with family and friends in attendance, they'd exchanged vows and she'd become Brynn Guyer. Leaving the Windham surname had been her choice.

But standing next to his wife, walking with her at the Beijing Opening Ceremonies, would be a close second to their wedding day.

Someone shouted U-S-A. Others joined in the cheer, including Brynn.

She looked up at him with an expression full of love. "We did it."

For nearly three years, they'd worked and trained together to get to this point. He'd thought he needed to do everything on his own to make it, but Chas had been correct. Being with Brynn and working to make both their dreams come true was a million times better. It hadn't been easy—both had faced setbacks—but neither had let the other give up. They'd pushed each other to do their best, always nearby with love when things didn't go well and to celebrate when their plans worked out. He wouldn't have wanted it to be any other way.

Satisfaction flowed through him. Ry kissed the top of her head. Well, her hat. "We did. And now we get to see what happens on the mountain."

"You mean, we go for the gold." Confidence overflowed. "Win."

"Yes." Only something changed for Ry on his journey to Beijing. The gold medal that had once been the driving force in his life was still part of his dreams, but if it came down to only one of them winning, he'd rather have Brynn wearing the medal than him. Oh, he'd give Chas a run for first place and knew in his heart he could beat his longtime friend and competitor, but Ry wanted to see his wife atop the podium with the National Anthem playing. She'd worked nonstop to make it back on the team. Winning would mean everything to her, and to him.

The signal to go was given.

Brynn let go of him. "This is it."

She was it. He held her hand. "Enjoy every second."

He gave her one more kiss, wanting to savor her sweet lips but knowing their team was moving.

Ry had thought nothing would be more

important than racing and winning a gold medal, but Brynn was. Competing at these Winter Games would be thrilling—a dream come true. But whatever happened would be icing on the cake. He'd won what was most important in life…her love. And he would cherish that—and her—forever.

Books in the One Night to Forever series:
Fiancé for the Night
The Wedding Lullaby
A Little Bit Engaged

You can find purchase information on my website here:
melissamcclone.com/FFTN

TO HEAR ABOUT FUTURE RELEASES, SIGN UP
FOR MY NEWSLETTER!

I send newsletters a few times each month with info
about new releases, sales, freebies, and giveaways. To
subscribe, go to www.subscribepage.com/mm_signup.

IF YOU ENJOYED READING THIS BOOK,
PLEASE LEAVE A REVIEW.

Honest reviews by readers like yourself help bring
attention to books. A review can be as short or as
detailed as you like. Thank you so much!

About the Author

USA Today bestselling author Melissa McClone has written over forty-five sweet contemporary romance novels and been nominated for Romance Writers of America's RITA® Award. She lives in the Pacific Northwest with her husband, three children, two spoiled Norwegian Elkhounds, and cats who think they rule the house. They do! If you'd like to learn more about Melissa, please visit www.melissamcclone.com or email her at melissa@melissamcclone.com. You can find Melissa on Facebook at melissamcclonebooks and her McClone Troopers Reader Facebook Group or connect with her on Twitter @melissamcclone and Instagram @melmcclone

Other Books by Melissa Mcclone

STANDALONE

The Christmas Window
A matchmaking aunt wants her nephew
to find love under the mistletoe…

SERIES
**All series stories are standalone,
but past characters may show up.**

Mountain Rescue Series
Finding love in Hood Hamlet
with a little help from Christmas magic…
His Christmas Wish
Her Christmas Secret
Her Christmas Kiss
His Second Chance
His Christmas Family

One Night to Forever Series
Can one night change your life…
and your relationship status?
Fiancé for the Night
The Wedding Lullaby

Beach Brides & Indigo Bay Sweet Romance Series
A mini-series within two multi-author series…
Jenny
Sweet Holiday Wishes
Sweet Beginnings

Quinn Valley Ranch
Relatives in a large family find love in Quinn Valley,
Idaho…
Carter's Cowgirl

Ever After Series
Happily ever after reality TV style…
The Honeymoon Prize
The Cinderella Princess
Christmas in the Castle

Love at the Chocolate Shop Series
Three siblings find love thanks to
Copper Mountain Chocolate…
A Thankful Heart
The Valentine Quest
The Chocolate Touch

The Bar V5 Ranch Series
Fall in love at a dude ranch in Montana…
Home for Christmas
Mistletoe Magic
Kiss Me, Cowboy
Mistletoe Wedding
A Christmas Homecoming

Made in the USA
Las Vegas, NV
17 April 2022

47614970R00166